A Summer with Dean

MICHAEL MCILWEE

Cover design and illustration by Gowtham Thangaraj.

First Edition: February 2026

Printed in the United States of America.

ISBN 979-8-218-92596-3 (paperback)

ISBN: 979-8-218-92595-6 (ebook)

To Mom, Tish, and Mair—thank you for teaching me to see the beauty in love, to hear the music in laughter, and to find grace in life's beautiful complexities.

To Jordy, for introducing me to Waterloo Sunset and for being the coolest guy I've ever met.

And to my dog Alfie, for keeping me company through every word of this book. You are a very good boy and have earned all the treats.

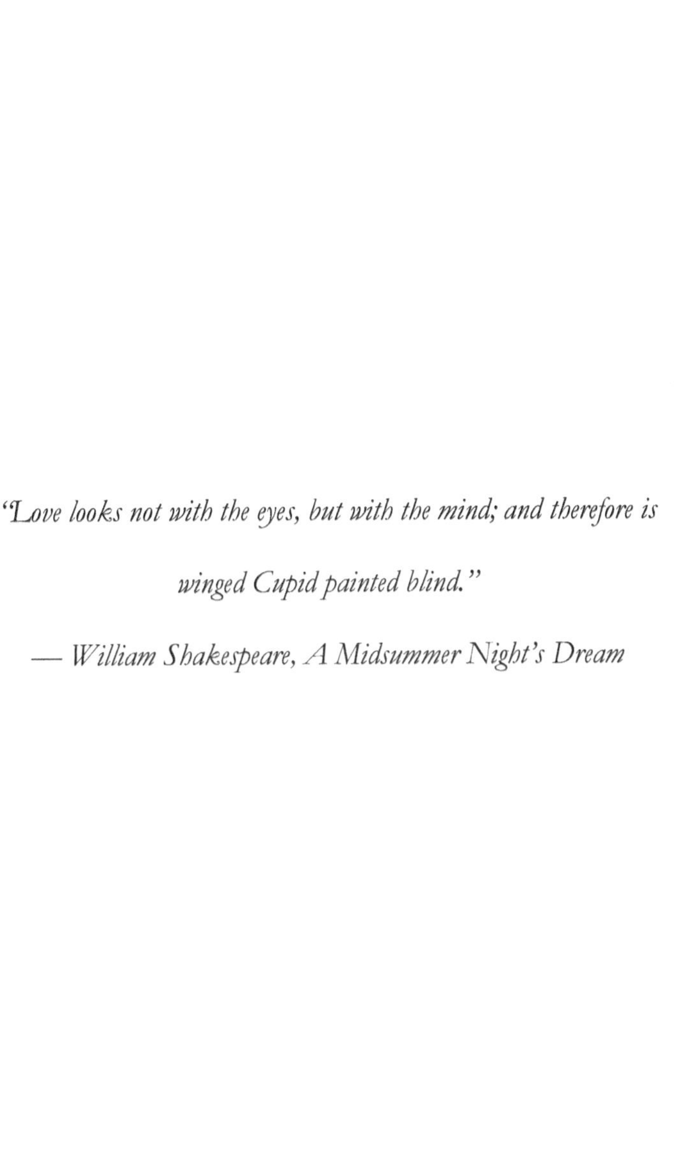

"Love looks not with the eyes, but with the mind; and therefore is

winged Cupid painted blind."

— William Shakespeare, *A Midsummer Night's Dream*

CHAPTER 1

Patrick looked up from the worn pages of his paperback copy of *Hamlet*. A shadow fell across his page, dimming the faint sunlight that filtered through the budding branches. He smiled faintly, expecting the familiar nod from the Central Park guitarist, as permanent as the bench he sat on. His brain, ever the optimist, had already filed this interaction under reliably safe—a rare, beautiful thing in this city.

The man's denim jacket looked like it had seen more seasons than Patrick had years. The color had given up the fight, faded into something between sky blue and storm gray, and the cuffs were frayed in a way that suggested not just wear but devotion. His face was a roadmap of sun and weather, creased in ways that told a story Patrick couldn't begin to read, the kind that suggested nights spent under open skies or maybe just a stubborn refusal to buy sunscreen. The beard alone looked like it could write a memoir.

Usually, the guitarist strummed through a well-worn set of Beatles classics, a quiet, soulful fixture of "Strawberry Fields," a human jukebox of peace and love. Patrick had been coming here long enough that he supposed he was a fixture now too, like the "Imagine" mosaic itself. He'd even started to notice the guitarist's small tells: the slight shoulder slump on colder days, the almost imperceptible bounce in his knee when a perfect song flowed from his fingers. Rituals like this were a comfort in a city that often felt like a relentless, unpredictable tide. The city was a storm—Strawberry Fields, a harbor.

It was one of the few places where Central Park unfurled like a perfectly ironed, lush blanket over the city's concrete bones. Tourists laid flowers on the mosaic, guitarists plucked familiar tunes, and the occasional New Yorker came to escape Manhattan's glorious, relentless chaos. For a fleeting moment, the concrete jungle remembered how to breathe. Even the distant sirens softened, blending into the city's symphony instead of shattering it.

Patrick leaned back, listening. His pale skin was already pinking slightly in the brisk wind. He blinked against the glare with green eyes that usually caught everything, watching pigeons coo and shuffle. Wind carried the faintest smell of roasted nuts from a street cart on Central Park West. New York was never quiet, not truly, but here it had the decency to lower its voice.

"Any requests?" the guitarist asked again, voice low and surprisingly gentle for someone who spent his days serenading a concrete circle. He tilted his head, inviting more than a quick transaction.

Patrick blinked. Requests? That was new. Apparently, the universe was open to improvisation.

"'Beautiful Boy.' John Lennon," he said, surprising himself. A quiet, tender lullaby, not a crowd-pleaser. More confession than performance.

The guitarist's eyebrows shot up beneath a fringe of gray hair. A crinkly smile deepened the lines around his eyes, those lines speaking to countless sunsets witnessed from this very bench.

"Don't get that one very often. Must be a softie under all that New York hustle." His gaze carried a knowing amusement, as if he could see straight through Patrick's carefully assembled layers.

Patrick's mouth tipped into a small, wistful smile. He did hustle, though mostly to survive the subway. Still, the man wasn't wrong.

"My mom used to sing it to me when I was a baby." Sometimes she still did, when she thought he wasn't listening.

"You got it." The guitarist nodded, understanding passing between them. He settled back onto his bench, adjusted the worn strap, and began to strum. A quiet, tender melody filled the crisp March air. The notes shimmered, and for a moment, even the honks and sirens faded. A small, unexpected gift from the universe.

Patrick relaxed against cool metal and let the familiar melody wash over him. He closed his eyes and was tiny again, fresh from a bubble bath, wrapped in a towel, his mom's voice, sweet and a little off key, filling the bathroom. During bath time, she'd dry him and sing, "Darling, darling, darling, Patrick." For a while, he thought the song truly had his name in it. Eventually, he realized she was replacing Sean, John Lennon's son. Still, it made the song feel uniquely his.

These days he came alone to Strawberry Fields about once a week. It was a calming escape from the treadmill of auditions and overpriced lattes. He'd run lines, scribble in his journal, or people-watch and invent elaborate backstories.

The woman with the oversized sunglasses? Definitely on the run from a scandal involving a senator and a yacht. The jogger circling for the third time? Avoiding a breakup waiting at home. New York was a stage, and Patrick cast them all without their knowledge.

Sometimes he wondered if anyone was doing the same to him, watching from a bench, spinning stories. *There goes Patrick, the melancholy actor in waiting, rehearsing lines no one has asked him to say.* He liked the idea that he might already be someone's character sketch. It made the city feel less lonely.

Today he tried to focus on *Hamlet*, but his mind kept drifting. A few weeks earlier, he'd sent his application to the Royal Academy of Dramatic Art, more famously known as RADA, for its intensive summer Shakespeare program. Highly selective with a small but real chance of leading to a master's program invitation. He was waiting. Waiting for an acceptance letter that could change everything. The question mark over his future looked a lot like an intimidating British school.

After college he'd danced and performed in musicals: Broadway, touring productions, a life he'd once dreamed of. He had the body for it—slim, toned, built for discipline. Yet from the wings, he'd often watched a lead pour his soul into an eleven o'clock number or a searing monologue. In those moments, he felt a gnawing desire for something deeper than physical storytelling. He felt the old sting of being the "background," a feeling he knew too well. Patrick wanted to push himself, to step out of the ensemble and prove he was an actor who could command the room with his voice, not just his movement. It was time to branch out, to challenge himself, to step outside what he knew.

He imagined delivering a powerful soliloquy, maybe with the slightest dramatic British lilt, captivating an audience not with a high kick but with the raw power of voice and emotion. He pictured himself center stage, lights burning hot, silence hanging thick, and his voice cutting through with something ancient and true. He wanted to feel the words take root in his chest and spill out uncontainable. The thought sent a quiet thrill through him. He wanted that risk, that rush.

His phone vibrated against his thigh.

Jonathan.

Jonathan was objectively hot and conversationally limited. A perfectly wrapped gift box filled with packing peanuts. Visually appealing, ultimately empty. Patrick sighed.

Jonathan: *Are we still on for a movie at my place tonight?*

Patrick: *Yeah, that works for me. You said you have a cat, right? I'm slightly allergic, just FYI.*

He was already planning an escape route: feigned hives, a dramatic fainting spell, perhaps a cough and a wheeze. He was a performer; commitment to the bit was his superpower.

Jonathan: *Yeah, I do. But I can keep him in another room. Wanna say 8:00?*

Patrick: *Ok, sounds good. See you then.*

Patrick set the phone down, the screen going dark, the conversation heavier than it should be. His dating record in New York wasn't great. He was picky. He didn't want the endless carousel of hookups; he wanted a classic fall-deep-and-hard romance. Witty banter. Shared glances across crowded rooms. Not another comment about "dancer legs" and flexibility.

He'd met interesting men and some truly bizarre ones. He'd considered changing his profile to: Seeking someone who won't fall in love with someone else mid-appetizer or fall asleep by dessert. Bonus if you can talk about something besides your gym routine or your ex's questionable choices.

Patrick remembered a date where, mid-appetizer, the guy had stared at him with apologetic eyes, taken a breath, and blurted, "I'm so sorry to do this, but I'm actually in love with someone else," then left him alone at the table. He'd been glad he could catalyze the man's emotional clarity. Noble, if humiliating. Maybe he was a lucky penny for other people's love lives. A romantic catalyst who helped others find their happily-ever-afters. Exhausting, but at least he was doing the universe a service.

He even joked once that he should start invoicing men for "emotional labor." First-date therapy: $100 per session. Heartbreak not included.

Jonathan, at least, was handsome. A good kisser. Possibly narcoleptic but confident and by Patrick's recently lowered standards, a gentleman, kinder than some others. Rough around the edges, like he'd stepped from a '90s indie film to play a brooding artist who finds redemption in a dusty record store. The cat was a problem, yes, but he could weather hives to break his losing streak. There was something intriguing about Jonathan, a brooding quality that tugged despite better judgment.

Patrick wanted the storybook romance more with each passing year: the click, the banter, the charged glances. He watched a couple across the path, hands clasped, oblivious to the world, and longed for that. Meet-cute, not meet-awkward-then-ghosted or meet-and-realize-you-love-someone-else.

His phone rang—FaceTime. LaShelle. His NYU best friend, ride-or-die, personal dating therapist, and designated emergency escape route.

They'd bonded at NYU over countless rewatchings of *Titanic* and *Mrs. Doubtfire*, screaming, "It was a run-by fruiting!" down the hallways at two in the morning. Monday nights were sacred: pints of Ben & Jerry's in their laps, yelling "Live from Hollywood!" with the *Dancing with the Stars* announcer. She knew his dating history better than anyone and had long campaigned for "nicer and out" guys. Translation: not emotionally unavailable cat-owning werewolves.

"Hey, stranger," she said as her face filled the screen. Even through the pixels, LaShelle radiated energy. Her black braids were woven with hints of red that caught the light, framing a face that was pure warmth. She had her oversized sunglasses perched on top of her head, and her smile was bright enough to cut through the overcast afternoon.

"Still at your little John Lennon shrine? It's practically snowing here." Her voice was a warm, familiar balm that cut through the city's hum.

"Always," he said, angling the phone so she could see the guitarist, a lone figure against the darkening sky. Streetlights flickered on, casting an ethereal glow through the budding branches. "Just waiting on RADA. My fate hangs in the balance, Shell. Pray for me. And send snacks. Comfort snacks. Winter is coming."

LaShelle's eyes narrowed playfully. "Oh, Winter is coming, is it? Did you find a direwolf in Central Park or just another bad date?" Mock sincerity wrapped around genuine excitement. She was his biggest cheerleader, even when he was a dramatic mess.

"I'm trying not to get my hopes up," he lied.

"Speaking of trying… Third date with Jonathan tonight." He braced for impact.

Her expression shifted to the familiar blend of exasperation and concern. "Him? Patrick, why are you still going out with that man? He sounds like a walking red flag convention, full parade, marching band, confetti made of your shattered dreams. He also seems chronically averse to staying awake." She took a beat. "You have a type, and that type is men who should come with a warning label and a complimentary sleep apnea machine. You're a moth to a flame, if the flame flickers and sometimes goes out mid-sentence."

"He's not that bad," Patrick hedged. "He's handsome. My type."

"Your type is 'handsome, a little rough around the edges, never asks about your day, and owns a deeply unsettling sleep schedule,'" she countered, smirking. "What about that nice accountant from the bar? He sent you flowers. Flowers, Patrick. Not a vague text about a cat."

"He was too nice," Patrick mumbled. "And his snort-laugh was like a walrus trying to start a chainsaw. Once I heard it, I couldn't unhear it. It haunted me."

"You're hopeless." She shook her head. "Alright, the code still stands. If it goes south, and by 'south' I mean anything less than a fairy-tale ending, text me: "Help is on the way, dear!'"

He laughed, tension loosening. "Already contemplating it, in case the cat gets brave or, you know, he falls asleep. Again."

"Good. Also, for the record, if RADA doesn't accept you, I'm flying to England to burn London to the ground."

"Subtle, Shell."

"Subtlety is for people without range. Love you. Text me."

"Love you too." The screen went black. He tucked the phone away, still smiling.

The sky had darkened, and the air sharpened. Forecast said snow, a late-season storm, heavy and wet, the kind that turned the city to slush overnight. He shivered and pulled his jacket tight, already imagining the story he'd tell

LaShelle if the night went sideways.

Man braves blizzard, narcoleptic date, and cat allergy for love. Pulitzer material.

By the time he reached the subway, the first flakes had started to fall, heavy and wet, sticking instantly to the sidewalks. City lights blurred into soft halos through the snowfall, turning Manhattan into an impressionist painting left out in the rain. His boots squeaked against wet concrete as he hurried toward the stairs.

Uptown to Washington Heights. Toward whatever storm waited, weather or otherwise.

It was precisely eight o'clock when Patrick reached Jonathan's apartment building, a nondescript stack of brick and fire escapes tucked off a narrow side street in Washington Heights.

Snow was coming down harder now, a thick, swirling blanket that softened the sidewalks and cars, muting honks and shouts into an eerie hush. Patrick hunched against the wind, grateful for the layers he'd piled on, though icy gusts still found their way through seams and collars, needling bone deep. He tugged his scarf higher, chin buried in wool, breath blooming into clouds that hung like impatient sighs. The storm felt relentless, the city reshaping itself into a frozen maze he wasn't sure he'd escape.

He took a steadying breath, trying to quiet the flutter under his ribs. Surely, he could handle Jonathan. Third-date territory was supposed to mean progress, not a battlefield. He muttered a silent prayer to the dating gods. *Please don't be a serial killer. Or a cat hoarder. Or both.*

The vestibule buzzer resisted his gloved finger before letting out a faint electronic hum, the lock clicking open like a dying robot's sigh. Inside, the heat hit him in a suffocating wave. The old-building smell clung to every wall: boiled cabbage from some neighbor's dinner, fried onions, and because fate hated him, a faint undercurrent of cat. His nose began to itch in anticipatory rebellion. Terrific. He'd be awkward and sniffly. Multi-tasking king. He was already imagining LaShelle's running commentary: "Oh, sure—nothing says sexy like sneezing into your date's face. Really locks the deal in."

The elevator was as ancient as the brickwork, groaning awake and hauling him upward with mechanical complaints. Patrick peeled off his gloves, fingers stiff from the cold, and tried smoothing his hair. Futile. Wind and snow had already styled it into "lost fight with snowdrift." He glanced at his reflection in the metal doors, which warped his face into a funhouse caricature: nervous eyes, crooked scarf, a man seconds away from deciding this was all a mistake.

When the elevator doors opened, Jonathan was waiting in the hallway. And damn if he didn't look exactly as advertised: tall, broad-shouldered, dark hair artfully mussed into just-rolled-out-of-bed perfection. His T-shirt clung just enough, soft and worn, and his jeans had that broken-in ease that screamed casual cool. It tugged at Patrick's traitorous stomach even as his brain whispered caution.

"Hey, come in," Jonathan said, stepping aside with an easy grin. His voice was low, warm, molasses smooth. "Snow's really coming down. Thought you might've turned into an icicle."

"Feels like December," Patrick answered, stomping snow from his boots, trying not to detonate an indoor weather event across the mat.

The apartment was textbook bachelor pad: glow of a big TV, a couch with cushions that had clearly survived pizza nights and questionable decisions, a scatter of remotes, a few wrappers. Not spotless, not catastrophic. Comfortably lived in. And, praise be, no cat in sight. Maybe his sinuses would survive. His shoulders unclenched just a little.

Jonathan gestured toward the couch. "So, what do you want to watch?"

Patrick sat, careful to avoid any popcorn fossils, the cushions sighing under him. Jonathan began the remote dance, pressing buttons with intense focus that didn't yield results. Finally: "Ever seen *Eyes Wide Shut*?" A glint in his eye Patrick couldn't quite read.

"Yeah," Patrick said cautiously.

Was this a test? An attempt at depth? An actual obsession with masks and secret societies? He considered suggesting something lighter but decided against being high maintenance. Jonathan hit play. The uneasy strings of Kubrick's score seeped into the room, dread unfurling in Patrick's chest. Perfect soundtrack for rising panic.

Jonathan slid an arm around him. The gesture landed like a misplaced limb. Third date, not decade-long marriage, Patrick reminded himself. He tried to breathe, to exist normally, to not transform into a human plank under the weight of that arm. Totally fine. Casual. Nothing to see here. *Stage direction: Patrick attempts a subtle shift; fails; contemplates life choices.*

Ten minutes in, a sound began, soft, rhythmic. A low rumble that blossomed into a full-bodied snore.

Patrick turned his head slowly, half-expecting a motorized animal hidden under the cushions. Nope. Jonathan. Out cold. Head tipped on Patrick's shoulder, mouth slack, each exhale a faint whistle like a tired kettle begging for mercy.

Eyes wide shut. Patrick wide awake.

Of course.

Jonathan shifted, let out a startled snort like a piglet caught mid-sneeze, and blinked awake. He stretched, catlike, as if the nap had been intentional. Lazy smile. "Sorry. Long day. Wanna...go to the bedroom?"

Patrick blinked. That was the pivot? From REM cycle to seduction? His brain scrambled. Bedroom. Sex. Or sleep. Or both? He weighed his options: brave a storm biblical enough to inspire new commandments or lean into absurdity.

"Sure," he heard himself say, detached like some other version of him had taken the wheel.

The bedroom was overheated to sauna levels, radiator roaring like an angry jet engine. A lamp glowed against sheets so crisp they looked ironed by angels. Patrick tugged at his collar, already sweating. His shirt clung in the worst way.

They kissed. And despite everything, the furnace, the nerves, the snoring interlude, Jonathan was good. Focused. Hungry. For a moment, sensation blurred doubt. Patrick gave in, his body remembering how to want, how to forget.

Then, mid-kiss, Jonathan slowed. Lips grazed once, twice...and his breathing shifted. Evened.

A soft snore slipped out.

Patrick froze.

No. No, no, no.

Jonathan had fallen asleep. Mid-makeout.

Patrick's eyes locked on the ceiling. Sweat dripped down his temples. He was trapped under a muscular arm that might as well have been wrought iron. A delicate roll failed; the arm clamped tighter. *This is how I die*, he thought. Suffocated by unconscious affection in a stranger's sauna-bedroom.

Minutes dragged. Twenty? Forty? His phone was out of reach. No LaShelle rescue text. The sacred Mrs.

Doubtfire code would have to wait. He imagined the headlines: PROMISING ACTOR FOUND DEAD UNDER MAN, CAUSE OF DEATH: BOREDOM AND SWEAT.

Miraculously, Jonathan stirred, stretching, yawning, blinking awake like Snow White's least punctual prince. And without missing a beat, resumed kissing. Urgency returned, and shirts hit the floor.

Patrick tried to surrender, to live in the moment. He could live with heat. With weird sleep cycles. Even with faint cat tang in the sheets. *This is fine. Salvageable. Don't overthink it.*

But then something shifted.

The sweat slicking their skin felt wrong. Thicker. Stickier. A metallic tang pricked his tongue. Sharp. Unmistakable. His stomach dropped.

"Hey," he rasped. "Could you, uh, turn on the light?"

Jonathan fumbled for the lamp.

Warm yellow flooded the room.

Patrick's gaze snapped to the mirror. His reflection stared back, smeared in dark red. Chest. Neck. Face. For a wild second: *Please, God, chocolate.*

It was not chocolate.

It was blood.

Patrick's scream tore out before he realized he was screaming.

"Oh. My. Fucking. God!"

Three detonations, loud enough to wake the neighbors, summon pigeons, and alert the gods themselves that New York dating had officially broken him.

Jonathan jerked upright, disoriented, hands flying to his face. The geyser of blood spraying from his nose looked less like a medical issue and more like a Tarantino prop malfunction. Thick crimson poured down his chin, soaking sheets, splattering Patrick's chest in wild arcs.

"I...I really need to use the bathroom," Patrick said, excusing himself as politely as he could, given the circumstances. He didn't wait for a reply, practically vaulting out of the bed, a new Olympic sport that involved dodging bodily fluids and maintaining a semblance of composure while internally screaming. This was less an exit and more a full-blown shitfit in motion.

He practically stumbled into the bathroom, flipping on the light with a trembling hand. He gasped, jumping back from his own reflection, a full-body flinch. He looked like something out of a Stanley Kubrick film—his second one of the night, no less—as if *The Shining*'s elevator had just decided to dump its entire contents directly onto him. Streaks of dark, clotted blood matted his hair, smeared his face, and crisscrossed his chest, a horrifying, sticky mask.

He quickly turned on the shower, not even bothering to wait for the water to warm up, and stepped in, scrubbing frantically, trying to rinse off as much of the sticky, horrifying mess as he could. The cold water shocked him, but he barely registered it over the pounding in his head and the frantic urge to be clean. He scrubbed until his skin was raw, but he didn't care. He didn't even manage to get all of it before the thought of Jonathan's bloody sheets sent him into a fresh wave of nausea.

Jonathan's muffled voice came through the door, sheepish. "It's the heat—the dryness. It happens all the time."

All the time? Patrick blinked in disbelief at the mirror fogging over. Netflix, chill, arterial spray? Hazmat team, priest, burn the sheets, his brain shrieked.

Patrick finally staggered out, damp, hastily pulling his shirt back on. Jonathan stood in the hall with a tissue wad pressed against his nose, still apologizing, still bleeding.

"I should, um... I should head home. Big day tomorrow."

Jonathan's face fell. "This doesn't usually happen this bad."

Patrick forced a hostage-negotiator smile. "It's fine. Really. Don't worry."

Translation: Never speaking of this again.

By the time the door shut, he was already halfway down the hall, desperate for cold air.

Outside, the storm swallowed him whole. Snowdrifts to his knees. Wind knifing exposed skin. Ice crystals lashing his cheeks. The city erased under a white curtain. He trudged blindly, following the dim glow of streetlights.

Each step, punishment. Boots filled with snow, socks iced stiff. He muttered under his breath, half-curse, half-prayer. "Never again. No more dating app. Silence. Chastity. Anything but this."

The wind howled louder, as if mocking him. He imagined monks trudging through snowdrifts in their long robes, solemnly nodding as they passed him, whispering in Latin about the fool who thought a third date might end in romance rather than a full-blown bloodbath. He nearly laughed, the image so vivid, his chest aching from it. He pictured himself taking vows, swearing allegiance not to God but to the noble art of never downloading Tinder again.

He pressed forward south toward his apartment. Salvation.

At one point he ducked into a shuttered bodega's awning just to catch his breath. The snow clung to his coat in icy clumps, soaking through. He rubbed his arms, shivering, then glanced into the darkened windows. He could just make out shelves lined with cans, chip bags, and, mocking him, rows of bottled water. His throat was parched, his body aching, and he wondered how absurdly dramatic he looked—a lone man standing outside a locked bodega at midnight, drenched in sweat, blood, and snow.

He wanted to bang on the glass and beg the ghosts of snacks to adopt him. Maybe this was it; maybe he'd freeze here and be discovered centuries from now, perfectly preserved between the Funyuns and the Twinkies, New York's own cautionary exhibit: *The Last Gay on Earth*. At this point, even a haunting would've been company. A bodega poltergeist. A spectral bag of Doritos whispering, "You good, babe?"

As he walked he thought of LaShelle. How she would howl when he told her. He could already hear her texts: Patrick, only you could turn a date into *Carrie: The Musical*. He smiled faintly, imagining her commentary in real time. Boy, you don't need the Royal Academy; you need an exorcist. Her voice in his head was warm, grounding, like a lifeline through the storm.

And then, suddenly, it wasn't just her voice he imagined but the weight of his own hopes pressing in. His phone buzzed faintly. He pulled it out with stiff fingers. Screen flared to life.

One new email.

"Royal Academy of Dramatic Art, Application Decision."

The storm hushed.

His thumb hovered. Breath shallow. This was it, the moment that might redraw his entire map. For a second the screen didn't load. Or maybe it did. He couldn't tell. The words swam, sharp and unreadable. What if it was a no? What if—

"We are delighted to inform you..."

Accepted.

He read it twice. A third time. The words blurred. Not snow, not wind—tears. A sound escaped, half laugh, half sob, echoing into the storm.

"Yes!" he shouted, arms flung wide. Snow caught in his hair, clung to his coat. He spun once, giddy, uncaring if any neighbor thought him mad. "YES!"

The blood, the furnace, the snoring disaster—all of it washed away. The storm no longer felt cruel but cleansing, a stage curtain parting on a new act. London.

He pressed his phone to his chest, heart pounding. For once he didn't care about soaked boots or frozen cheeks. For once everything felt exactly as it should.

Patrick trudged south with buoyancy in his step, snow swirling like confetti. Alone, frozen, but certain. The next chapter of his life had just begun.

And maybe, just maybe, London would be a place where the only thing gushing was his talent, and the only unexpected fluid was a perfectly brewed cup of tea.

A boy could dream.

CHAPTER 2

Patrick got to his apartment just as the storm clenched tighter around the city. He leaned his weight into the door until it closed with a dull *thunk*, sealing him off from the blizzard's howl. Cold seeped through his coat, a bizarre counterpoint to the feverish heat still lingering on his skin. Jonathan's heat. Jonathan's blood. Jonathan's fucking cat. His cheek was sticky, his clothes still carried that iron tang.

Home sweet home: snow, dried blood, existential dread. A look he would not recommend, even to his worst enemy.

The apartment door clicked shut behind him, the sound impossibly loud in the sudden quiet. Outside, the blizzard staged a white-knuckled coup, mirroring the chaos still ricocheting around his skull like a rogue pinball.

He peeled off his snow-dusted coat and let it drop into a heap. The quiet apartment felt like a balm after the sensory overload of the last few hours. The only light came from the faint glow of streetlamps through snow-laden windows, casting the room in a muted pallor. The silence made the frantic thrum of his own pulse feel deafening.

He sank onto the couch, not even bothering to take off his boots, shivering, his whole body an instrument of exhaustion. He told himself he was fine.

This was New York, yes—a city famous for wild stories and eccentric characters. But even by New York standards, a date ending in a blood geyser was a new category of disaster. Not just "bad date." Something far worse. He was pretty sure his current situation was a clusterfuck no stage manager on earth could fix.

He needed a shower. Desperately. But first, he needed Eli.

He looked at the closed bedroom door of his roommate Eli, who was blissfully asleep. Usually, their end-of-day ritual involved ridiculous recaps of auditions, bizarre subway rides, or failed flirtations. He could already hear Eli's dramatic gasp, the perfectly timed horror, the inevitable cackle.

Patrick knocked. No answer. Louder. Nothing. Finally, with the rhythm of a desperate survivor, he pounded again.

A muffled groan. "What fresh hell is it, Patrick?" Eli's voice, thick with sleep, carried the weary cadence of a man too used to late-night emergencies.

"It's a fresh hell of the very bloody variety," Patrick whispered, leaning closer to the door. "I need you. And possibly a priest. And a hazmat suit."

There was rustling, a *thump*, and a curse. The door creaked open, revealing Eli. He stood there, tall and skinny, the quintessential "actor type" radiating a vibe of chaotic comfort. His hair was an explosion of curly bedhead that defied all physics, and he was dressed in his signature look: mismatched socks and an oversized t-shirt that hung loosely on his frame.

If anyone could talk him down from a blood-soaked spiral, it was Eli, dorky but cool, blanket clad and battletested. His blurry eyes widened. "Holy… What the fuck happened?"

Patrick gave a helpless laugh-sob. "Worse than you think. Couch. You won't believe it."

Eli, suddenly alert, followed him into the living room. He snapped on a lamp, wrapped himself in a blanket, and leaned forward, eyes sparkling. "Spill. Spare no gory detail."

Patrick relived it all. Eli gasped, laughed, clutched his blanket theatrically, his face caught between horror and pure entertainment. "Patrick, this isn't dating. This is guerrilla theater. You need hazard pay."

Patrick buried his face in his hands. "I swear, I'm going to need therapy. Or an exorcism. Maybe both."

Eli wiped his tears of laughter, but his voice softened. "Shower. Tea. Then we dissect the blood fountain. And after that, we find you a non-hemorrhaging date."

Patrick scrubbed with shampoo until his scalp tingled, muttering under the stream like a man desperate for absolution.

The water beat down like judgment, hot enough to sting, not hot enough to erase. He closed his eyes, and the night replayed itself in red: Jonathan snoring, Jonathan's furnace of an apartment, Jonathan's blood turning Patrick into collateral damage. He braced his forehead to the tile, laughter bubbling up against sobs.

This was his life. Absurd, catastrophic, and yet somehow still moving forward.

When he emerged, towel-wrapped and human-adjacent, Eli already had Earl Grey steeping, the aroma a comforting reminder of sanity. The apartment, moments ago bleak, now glowed warm again. Eli sat curled in his chair, phone in hand, no doubt already crafting a dramatic retelling for LaShelle.

Then he remembered. RADA. The email.

His heart skipped. His fingers trembled as he opened it. *What if this was a mistake? What if they meant to send this to Patrick O'Connell the dentist? Was there a dentist?* Shit, should he take up dentistry instead?

The words leapt: "delighted to confirm… accepted… 20 June through 30 August."

Beneath, a line that seemed to glimmer with grandeur: "Patron: His Majesty the King. Founded by Sir Herbert Beerbohm Tree, 1904."

He tossed the phone to Eli, who shrieked, then lunged into a celebratory hug. They danced like fools, tea sloshing, shouting, laughing until their sides hurt.

RADA. London. Shakespeare. And now, somehow, Patrick was joining their ranks. It felt impossible and undeniable all at once. A door had opened. Through it, a future.

Eli's eyes were still wide, darting between Patrick and the glowing phone screen. "Patrick, do you realize what this means? You're going to walk the same halls as Anthony Hopkins. You're going to rehearse on the very stages that trained Alan Rickman!"

Patrick laughed, breathless, almost disbelieving. "I kept telling myself it was a long shot. Just something to say I tried. I'm actually going to London. I'm going to stand on those stages, speak those words. Shakespeare." His voice cracked on the last word, equal parts awe and terror.

Eli threw his blanket dramatically over one shoulder like a cape. "We're not just talking about a summer. We're talking about the launch of Patrick O'Connell: International Man of Theater. I want your autograph now before you forget your humble roommate when you're too busy having tea with Dame Judi Dench."

Patrick grinned, but tears pricked his eyes. He thought of the countless nights pacing lines in this very living room, of the auditions that ended in silence, of the plays he'd poured himself into in basements and black boxes across the city. All of it had been leading here.

"I feel like if I blink, it'll disappear. Like it's too good to be real."

Eli sat beside him, clutching his arm. "It is real. And you've earned every letter in that email. You've bled for this city—literally tonight, which is poetic in a very gross way. You've chased it, and it's here."

Patrick laughed, wiping his face. The blizzard raged outside, but inside he was warm, lit by possibility.

Eli wasn't finished. He leaned in, voice dropping to a conspiratorial hush. "And RADA isn't just any school. It's the crucible. You'll be training with voices that shake stone walls. Movement classes that break you down and rebuild you like steel. Every day you'll be in rooms that still echo with centuries of theater. People dream their whole lives for that chance. And you, Patrick O'Connell from Scranton, just got handed the key."

Patrick blinked, the words sinking in with a weight heavier than the snowstorm outside.

"I don't know, Eli. Part of me is terrified I'll walk in there, and they'll all know instantly that I don't belong."

Eli scoffed and swatted his shoulder with the blanket. "Bullshit. You've got the hunger. You've got the fight. It is about stripping you bare and finding out what's underneath, and what's underneath you is grit and spark and a sense of humor twisted enough to survive geyser-nose Jonathan. Trust me, Patrick. You'll belong the second you step into that rehearsal room."

Patrick let himself breathe, a shaky, uneven sound. He sipped his tea, letting Eli's words wash over him. For the first time, he allowed himself to imagine it in detail: the old rehearsal halls, the smell of dust and polish, the clatter of students reciting Shakespeare in accents sharp and strange. He pictured himself there, not as an imposter but as a participant. As someone meant to be shaped by that fire.

The thought made his chest ache with a joy so fierce it bordered on pain.

As he sat there, the email still glowing in his mind, his thoughts spilled outward like a stage light hitting dusty velvet. One moment he was staring at Eli's grin, the next he was tumbling down a corridor of memory. His mind wandered backward.

He felt the letter's glow pull him back to the first spark: Aunt Ann tugging his tiny hand, dragging him into New York's neon blaze. Times Square, pretzels, ambition, noise. The Majestic Theatre's velvet seats, the chandelier of *Phantom* crashing, music thundering through his bones. He'd been six, yet he knew: Theater would be his life. He'd lived the rest of the show on the edge of his seat, already imagining himself in a cape, singing to the rafters.

After his parents' divorce, his mother and her sisters Ann and Therese were his anchors. They'd cheered his every performance, no matter how makeshift. They were his confetti-throwing fan club, their unwavering support stitched into his bones.

The thought of those Broadway nights carried him homeward in memory: Scranton, Pennsylvania, the Electric City. A small town where gossip moved faster than buses. Patrick had turned it into his stage: class president, prom king, clarinetist, drama nerd. He'd lived for choir rehearsals, band competitions, and plays where he always angled for the juiciest role.

Vanessa and Brigid had been his tribe, his co-conspirators. Brigid across the street, host of midnight marathons, karaoke nights, and fridge raids. Vanessa, locker neighbor, sarcastic soulmate, the first person he'd told the truth to.

High school had been contradictions—outwardly confident, inwardly uncertain. He'd dated girls, smiled for prom photos, but felt himself drawn to boys. He was a nerd. He watched *Star Wars* and stared longer at Harrison Ford than Carrie Fisher. His first kiss was with Chuck, the valedictorian of his class. They couldn't stand each other, but Patrick had realized he was the only option, using it as practice before returning to their mutual disdain.

By the time he'd reached college in New York, the thread of those memories had woven seamlessly into discovery. College and New York were revelations. A kaleidoscope of identities, freedom to experiment. Here, he knew. He wanted men. He wanted honesty. He wanted his life fully his.

He'd told Vanessa first over coffee at their favorite coffee shop, Northern Light, nervously fiddling with ladybug-stickered cups. Then Brigid during a movie marathon with a hand squeeze in wordless solidarity. Then his mom, whose tears and love spilled out at once.

Later, his dad. Surprisingly, coming out as gay hadn't been the battlefield Patrick feared. His dad had offered a gruff, quiet acceptance that felt like a miracle. No, the real war, the memory that still had teeth, had happened years earlier. It wasn't about boys; it was about ballet. He thought of the silence at sixteen, the months of dead air that followed his confession about wanting to dance professionally. He thought of the years of "tolerance" that had followed, the dismissive questions about when he would get a "real job," and how that silence had driven him to prove his worth every single day.

He looked down at the RADA acceptance letter. This wasn't just an invite to a school. It was the answer to that silence. London was his chance to finally stop proving himself to a ghost in his head and just *be*.

Each step, each confession, each cheer, each stumble, all of it had led him here, to Eli, to this moment, to this email glowing in the dim light of their apartment.

He thought of Aunt Ann buying him his first script, of Brigid and Vanessa screaming show tunes at his piano, of his mom crying when he landed his first lead. He thought of Scranton and its small-town gossip, of choosing theater instead of touchdowns. Of finally feeling free.

Patrick's thoughts carried him forward into a realm of possibility that felt almost frightening in its brightness. He imagined walking along the Thames, tracing the curve of the river where so many actors must have wandered, scripts clutched in cold hands. He pictured climbing narrow staircases in drafty old theaters, name taped above a rehearsal room door, his voice bouncing against centuries-old stone as he practiced iambic pentameter.

He could see himself fumbling with lines in front of classmates whose accents made the words sound like music, until slowly, he learned to match their rhythm. He imagined seeing his reflection in the foggy windows of the Tube, costume bag slung over his shoulder, whispering lines as strangers ignored him in true London fashion. A connection. A spark of the new life waiting for him there.

For the first time in a long while, the chaos inside him stilled. Ahead lay London, Shakespeare, possibility. The curtain was rising. And this time Patrick was ready.

But Patrick couldn't sleep. Not yet. He lay back on the couch, staring at the ceiling, letting the storm's muffled roar seep in through the windows. He replayed Jonathan's geyser episode, Eli's laughter, and the email's electric words until they blurred together in a surreal montage.

He found himself pacing again, restless energy flooding his system. He opened his worn notebook, the one crammed with half-formed monologues, scribbled ideas, overheard subway dialogues, and started to write. He didn't know what. Just lines, fragments. A storm inside, meeting the storm outside. His words tumbled out, clumsy but alive.

When he paused, Eli's soft snoring drifted from the bedroom. The apartment was still, the storm a lullaby, and Patrick smiled faintly.

And with that, he finally let sleep claim him. Outside, the storm still raged. Inside, came stillness. Somewhere beyond the snow and subway, a future waited, curtain rising.

CHAPTER 3

A couple of months later, the May weather in New York City had finally shaped up, as if it had decided to torture its inhabitants enough for one spring. The biting winds of March were a distant, blood-splattered memory, and the city was blooming, bursting with a chaotic, vibrant energy.

Patrick found himself actually enjoying the commute, a rare and miraculous occurrence, as the subway cars no longer felt like mobile saunas and the sidewalks were clear of treacherous patches. Even the pigeons seemed to coo with a renewed sense of purpose, like they too had survived winter and were now out here trying to rebrand as emotionally available.

LaShelle and Patrick had decided it was the perfect day to go lay out in Central Park, a much-needed catch-up session under the glorious spring sun. They loved to spread out blankets, bringing dubious iced teas and suspiciously large bags of chips to bask in the rare luxury of catching some sun, a difficult feat in a city perpetually shadowed by skyscrapers and famously lacking in horizontal green space.

It felt, he thought, like an actual civilized way to spend an afternoon, especially compared to his recent dating adventures, which mostly involved dodging bodily fluids and existential dread. The air was soft, scented with freshly mown grass and distant cherry blossoms, a welcome break from the usual perfume of exhaust and ambition.

They found their usual spot near the Great Lawn, far enough from the bustling paths to feel private yet close enough to indulge in people-watching. With her usual efficiency, LaShelle unfurled a vibrant tie-dye blanket that seemed to drink in the sunlight, and they settled onto its soft expanse.

He pulled out his battered copy of Hamlet, but his mind was too restless to focus on Danish princes and existential crises. It kept drifting to London, to RADA, to the shimmering, uncertain future waiting for him.

"So, are you actually excited or just pretending for my benefit? Because your default setting is mildly anxious but trying to seem chill," LaShelle asked, adjusting her oversized sunglasses with mock skepticism. She popped a chip into her mouth, the crunch absurdly loud in the quiet of the park. Even behind the dark lenses, her eyes seemed to bore into him, demanding the truth.

He couldn't contain it. He was practically buzzing like a caffeinated hummingbird.

"Are you kidding? I'm shitting myself. It's RADA. I'm going to London. I'll be a proper actor. I'll wear tweed, say 'cheerio,' and develop a tea addiction so pretentious it'll require subtitles."

He threw his hands up, narrowly avoiding a passing jogger who, seemingly accustomed to Central Park theatrics, barely flinched.

LaShelle chuckled, a low, knowing sound that vibrated through the blanket.

"Just try not to find yourself another human blood fountain over there. Or, you know, a British prince. Honestly, I wouldn't be mad. Think of the stories. *American actor causes international incident with royal nosebleed.*" She fanned herself theatrically, already overwhelmed by the imagined scandal.

He rolled his eyes. "A prince? Please. With my luck he'd be allergic to me, or fall asleep during his coronation, or declare undying love for a distant cousin while eating a scone. My romantic life is a tragic comedy, Shell. No princes. Just...chaos."

"I am a monk now," he added, staring at the sky. "A celibate, artistic monk dedicated solely to the worship of Shakespeare. Men are distractions. I am married to the Bard."

He sighed. "I'm just hoping London offers a different flavor of disaster. Like accidentally insulting the king or mistaking a badger for a very fluffy dog."

As the afternoon sun dipped, casting long shadows across the Great Lawn and painting the sky in soft orange and rose, they packed with practiced efficiency, folded blankets, stuffed empty chip bags into a tote. The air cooled, carrying the faint, sweet scent of evening dew.

They headed toward Jacob's Pickles, one of their Upper West Side go-tos for comfort food and easy conversation, a place where the mac and cheese was legendary and the atmosphere welcoming. Inside, a warm hum of chatter and clinking glasses, a happy-hour symphony. The aroma of fried chicken and dill wrapped them in a comforting, greasy embrace that promised delicious calories and even better gossip.

They snagged two barstools, the worn wood sticky with ghosts of spilled drinks, and ordered their usual bottomless spiked strawberry lemonades. Some traditions were sacred, especially the ones involving sugar and questionable alcohol.

"I'm just gonna hit the ladies' room," LaShelle said, sliding off her stool with practiced ease, already scanning the room for potential drama. "Don't let anyone too interesting talk to you while I'm gone. You know how you get. And frankly, my emotional bandwidth for your dating debriefs is at an all-time low after that Jonathan incident."

She winked and disappeared into the throng, a blur of vibrant energy.

He rolled his eyes. "Please. Like anyone interesting ever

approaches me."

He watched her go and silently prayed no one too interesting would appear. His track record suggested otherwise.

He took a sip of his overly sweet lemonade, savoring the low hum of conversation, the clink of glass, the comforting smell of fried food. Peace, rare and brief, settled over him.

Then a voice beside him, smooth as aged whiskey, deep and resonant, said, "Hello."

He turned and promptly forgot how to breathe.

The man next to him was...beautiful. Not just handsome. Unfairly, jawline-like-a-weapon, shouldn't-be-allowed-in-public handsome. Patrick's brain short-circuited. His fight-or-flirt reflex activated. Flirt lost. Badly.

The man was offensive. That was the only word for it. He was offensively good-looking. He gave off a regal air. Rege-Jean Page but somehow more impossible, like a CGI rendering or a Greek god who'd wandered in for a pickle. His simple, well-tailored shirt (probably worth more than Patrick's entire wardrobe) clung just enough to hint at sculpted muscle. An immediate, visceral pull. Patrick felt the magnetic force bulldoze every carefully constructed wall of self-preservation. So much for the monk life. The monk had just defrocked himself.

"Hi," he managed, a little squeaky, betraying the sudden panic. His brain ran a quick diagnostic. Danger:

Hot Person Alert. Proceed with extreme caution. Or go full steam ahead. Who cared? The debate was fierce. Uncharacteristic bravery won. Another anecdote for LaShelle, worst case. He was practically collecting them.

"I'm Victor," the man said, extending a hand. As he did, his phone buzzed on the bar. He flipped it face-down with practiced ease, never breaking eye contact. The grip was firm, warm.

A wiser man might have called that a red flag, but Patrick was too busy drowning in Victor's gaze to notice. Patrick's palm felt suddenly inadequate, like a damp dish rag or a very small, very nervous theatrical prop.

"Patrick," he said, aiming for cool and collected while his heart attempted a full-blown Broadway tap number. He managed a small, hopefully charming smile, trying to project an air of casual confidence he definitely didn't feel.

They chatted for a couple of minutes, a polite exchange about surprisingly good bar snacks and the miraculous shift in the weather. Victor's voice was a low, melodic hum, a baritone that made Patrick want to lean in and absorb every syllable. The actual words mattered less than the sound like a perfectly tuned instrument.

Victor's phone buzzed again. He silenced it quickly, sliding it into his pocket with a faint, almost dismissive smile. "Sorry. Work stuff," he said smoothly, moving the conversation back to Patrick.

Patrick barely noticed, too dazzled by the fact that this

impossibly handsome man seemed intent on listening to him.

He was about to launch into a particularly embarrassing *Cats* audition story, specifically the part where his over-zealous Mr. Mistoffelees leap kicked over the casting table, headshots and resumes scattering like startled mice, a moment that still haunted his dreams, when LaShelle reappeared, sliding onto her stool with the stealth of a trained operative, eyes glinting with curiosity.

"And this is LaShelle," he said, introducing them, trying to keep his voice even as if he hadn't just had a minor existential crisis over a stranger's jawline. He begged her telepathically for a subtle, discreet assessment.

"Nice to meet you," Victor said, offering his hand. LaShelle's eyes, however, were already doing their wide-eyed, laser-focused evaluation: his hair, his shoes, the whole package—a silent interrogation that could rival the FBI.

Patrick felt her elbow nudge his ribs. Talk. He glanced over. She mouthed, exaggerated, "Is. He. Gay?"

LaShelle's eyebrows were now a Morse code of gaydar inquiry. Patrick's brain replied in static.

Heat rushed up Patrick's neck to his hairline. He shook his head minutely and mouthed back, "I. Don't. Know!"

He widened his eyes at her. *Help me*, he signaled. *Or kill me. Either is fine.*

They dissolved into silent giggles, masking it with

coughs and frantic sips, a masterclass in awkward social camouflage they'd perfected over years of theatrical mishaps and questionable dating choices.

Victor simply smiled, oblivious, or very, very good at pretending.

Conversation spun on—school, shared memories, the absurdities of New York, a city that never sleeps and never stops supplying material for their debriefs. Victor returned to his drink, still unruffled. Patrick kept stealing glances. The elegant curve of Victor's neck, his hand on the glass, the subtle line of muscle in his forearm. A work of art. A very distracting one.

Just as Patrick was about to deliver the spectacular conclusion to the *Cats* story, Victor leaned in, voice a smooth murmur. "So, what are you two doing after this?"

Patrick's mind went blank. His brain, trained by years of bad dates, hadn't even considered an after. Abort. Abort.

"Uh, nothing, really," he said, and instantly regretted it. He should have claimed plans, laundry, emergency houseplant surgery, training for the Olympic synchronized swimming team—anything but "nothing."

LaShelle, wing-woman in shining armor, pounced. "Oh, I actually have to get home. Work in the morning. Early call time. You know how it is."

She shot Patrick a look that screamed, "This is your chance. Do not screw it up." Under the bar, her foot found his, a not-so-gentle nudge. Move.

Patrick stared at her, wide-eyed, silently asking if she was serious. Abandoning him with Prince Charming? What if he was a serial killer? A very handsome serial killer but still.

LaShelle smiled sweetly at Victor, pure innocence. "But Patrick's free. He lives for an adventure. Or just someone to listen to his dramatic anecdotes."

Patrick swallowed, throat suddenly dry. "Yeah, sure. We could…do something," he said, aiming for casual while feeling like he'd been tossed into the deep end of the dating pool without floaties, a very attractive shark circling.

They paid quickly. LaShelle hugged him tight and whispered, in her best Robin Williams voice, "Help is on the way, dear. Text me every detail. And if he has a cat, you know the drill."

He giggled, too high-pitched for a grown man. "I'll text you later," he hissed back, already promising a forensic analysis of Victor's charm, potential serial-killer tendencies, and the precise trajectory of his jawline.

Outside, the air was crisp after the bar's warmth. The city sparkled under streetlights, a cinematic backdrop for the beginning of something new. The usual traffic cacophony felt like a gentle, rhythmic pulse, a soundtrack for a nascent connection.

"Would you like to take a walk to Central Park?" Victor asked, voice velvet smooth. Even in the dim light, his eyes carried an inviting warmth. Another buzz from his pocket. He ignored it, smile unwavering.

"I actually just came from there," Patrick admitted, a blush rising. "I basically live there. I am the phantom of the Great Lawn."

He wanted to die. *Phantom?* Why did he say that? Now he sounded like he lived in a sewer and kidnapped sopranos. He immediately wished a trap door would open beneath him.

Truth was, he would have walked to the moon if Victor asked, but he kept that to himself. "But I don't mind a stroll. It's beautiful out, like the city got a fresh coat of glitter after the rain."

They walked. Conversation flowed easily, a refreshing change from Jonathan's monologues, which had mostly consisted of snoring. The crisp night air was invigorating, a breath of fresh, non-bloody air. Damp grass cushioned their steps. Somewhere quiet by a small pond, they sat. The distant city hum and the occasional rustle of leaves framed the moment, a tiny pocket of stillness lit by far-off lamps reflecting on damp earth.

They told each other their stories in quick, overlapping beats. Patrick opened up, his theatrical ambitions, his quirky family, a self-deprecating joke about his knack for attracting dramatic situations. Victor listened closely, eyes bright with genuine interest, asking thoughtful questions, offering warm, measured reactions that made Patrick feel seen.

Victor had graduated from Princeton, political science, which explained the ease and precision in his voice and the quiet authority he carried. He spoke of his work with a calm passion Patrick found maddeningly attractive.

"I'm actually heading to London this summer for a program at University College London," Victor said, thoughtful gaze turned outward. "I'm considering law and want to see if studying there is the right path."

Patrick lit up like he'd downed five espressos and discovered a secret glitter reserve. The universe was playing a prank. A cruel, hilarious prank.

"I'm going to London this summer," he blurted, very golden retriever. Too perfect, too serendipitous, a cosmic alignment of flights and fledgling dreams.

Victor's eyebrow arched. "Really? That's great. What for?" His smile widened, real warmth spreading, though his hand twitched toward his pocket again when his phone buzzed.

"I got into RADA," Patrick said, grinning too big for his face. "It's right near UCL, practically down the street. We'll be neighbors. We can grab coffee or…whatever."

Destiny tugged at him, finally on his side, and sending him a very attractive consolation prize wrapped in a perfectly tailored shirt.

Emboldened by the shared destination (and his own audacity), he went for it. Life was short. He'd already survived a literal bloodbath.

"Hopefully we could see each other there," he said, trying to sound casual while internally planning an entire London itinerary. Shakespeare's Globe, tea shops, maybe even a clandestine brush with royalty. He took a breath. "Are you dating anyone?"

Victor held his gaze, a slow, deliberate connection.

"No," he said, the pause before his answer almost imperceptible. Then that small, knowing smile again, promising secrets and possibilities. "Are you?"

"No," Patrick answered, triumph warming his chest. "That's cool. I mean, great. That's really great to hear."

He mentally slapped himself. *Great to hear?* What the fuck was he saying?

"Well, you're very handsome," he added before he could overthink it. Sometimes you just had to leap. He felt a delicious thrill, daring, new, inexplicably calm.

Victor's smile widened, lighting his eyes. "So are you."

Sincere. Warm. It had nothing to do with leftover bar heat and everything to do with the surprise of being seen.

By then the park was dark, city noise a distant murmur, grass shimmering like a scatter of tiny diamonds under the streetlights. Alone on the bench, still air around them, the moment tightened and sweetened.

This time, no geysers. No ghosts. Just a quiet night and the terrifying possibility that something might actually go right.

Victor leaned in, closer, closer, and kissed him. Soft, tentative, a question. It tasted like expensive bourbon and bad decisions. Patrick answered, leaning in, and the kiss deepened, warm, lingering, promising.

Deep down, his survival instincts were screaming at him to *abort*, citing a historical crash-and-burn rate of one hundred percent. But for tonight, he decided to disconnect the alarm.

CHAPTER 4

The calendar flipped to June, and with it, a peculiar kind of magic settled over Patrick's life. It wasn't the sort that involved wands or enchanted castles but a very real, very potent spell, cosmic benevolence courtesy of Victor, a man who seemed to have stepped straight out of Patrick's most carefully curated daydreams.

If he were being honest, their actual dates were few and far between. Victor was elusive, a man perpetually "swamped with work" or "tied up with family obligations" that sounded vaguely royal. There were long stretches of silence between texts, days where Patrick checked his phone so often he developed a phantom vibration in his thigh. But Patrick didn't mind the scarcity. In fact, he romanticized it. It made their time together feel like a limited-edition print—rare, precious, and valuable because there wasn't enough of it.

When they *did* meet, the dates blurred into shared glances, whispered jokes, and the exhilarating discovery of new facets of each other. Victor was witty and intelligent, carrying a quiet confidence Patrick found irresistibly alluring, though sometimes it shaded into something closer to arrogance when Victor spoke at length about Princeton or his future in law.

Conversations flowed effortlessly, from political theory to the merits of various Broadway musicals, Victor listening intently, eyes bright with genuine interest. At other times, he checked his phone with a faint apologetic smile, sliding it back into his pocket as though nothing was wrong. Patrick noticed but dismissed it. He wanted the fantasy. He soaked in every moment. Was it a boyfriend? A situation-ship? A really intense cameo appearance in Patrick's life? It didn't matter. Patrick had memorized these tiny gestures, hoarding them like precious artifacts. Each became proof of something grander, confirmation that this time, finally, the universe had chosen to reward him.

When sex inevitably came, it was intense, passionate, and shockingly tender. It moved like a swift current pulling them along, and Patrick, usually cautious and prone to overthinking, let himself be swept away. Victor was attentive, intuitive. Every touch, every lingering kiss, felt like a quiet conversation, a deepening connection that eclipsed words. Victor was handsome, intelligent, and witty, and he seemed genuinely captivated by Patrick's chaotic charm, dramatic flair, and quirky observations. He had found him, the perfect guy. Or at least close enough to perfect.

He pictured their London life. Patrick, with his actor's imagination, filled in details: Victor laughing as rain poured and they huddled under one umbrella, late-night arguments about art in smoky pubs, lazy Sunday mornings tangled in bedsheets while the muffled city hummed below. He believed in it so fully it felt real already, as if his heart had simply leapt forward in time and decided to live there until his body caught up.

He began telling Eli about it in long, rambling voice notes, acting out entire conversations with Victor that hadn't happened yet. In his mind Victor was already an audience member at his first RADA showcase, clapping wildly, shouting his name, the kind of cinematic support that would turn any performance into a coronation. His chest swelled with the fantasy until it felt bigger than his body could contain.

One sweltering afternoon, in the days before departure, Patrick wandered into a small, quirky West Village shop he had never noticed. Tucked on a narrow cobblestone street, its dusty window was cluttered with antique curiosities. Inside, the place smelled of dust and forgotten adventures, melancholic yet inviting. In a glass case, glowing softly beneath a dusty lamp, lay two matching necklaces: simple, delicate silver chains, each with an intricate little compass charm. They weren't flashy, just elegant and understated, hinting at journeys and shared paths.

He smiled, thinking of Victor. Two people setting out on new journeys in a new city yet finding their way to each other. It felt right. He envisioned giving one to Victor, a quiet gesture, a promise to always find their way back. He bought them both, the cool weight in his palm feeling heavy and hopeful and tucked them into a velvet pouch deep in his carry-on: a secret talisman for his London future.

Later that week, on FaceTime with Victor, already in London, Patrick brought up his movie idea. "When I get there, if you're free, we could see a film. There's an old movie theater showing *The Empire Strikes Back*, the original. Classic. A perfect escape from the settling-in madness." He tried to sound casual, though his heart was doing a frantic jig.

Victor laughed, that deep, resonant sound that always sent a thrill through him. "I'll have to check my schedule once I'm settled, but that sounds great. Consider it a provisional date."

Provisional, he thought. A normal person might have heard "maybe." Patrick heard a blood oath.

Farewells in New York were a whirlwind of emotion, a chaotic symphony of tears, hugs, and last-minute advice. His mom and aunts, a tearful, loving trio, all but enveloped him at the airport, dispensing last tips about tea consumption and proper umbrella etiquette.

"Call us every day, Patrick!" his mother wailed, probably already planning her next pilgrimage to Strawberry Fields in his honor.

Aunt Ann pressed a twenty into his palm. "For emergencies. Or for a particularly strong gin and tonic. You'll need it. London's a grand old dame, but she can be a bit much."

Aunt Therese hugged him tight, whispering, "We are so proud of you. Go conquer the world." Their unwavering support was a comforting anchor in the chaos.

LaShelle and Eli, practical and dramatic respectively, staged a final debrief at their favorite coffee shop. LaShelle's eyes, usually sharp when judging his dating choices, were soft with genuine excitement. "Okay, look. You've got this. RADA is going to be incredible. And Victor…he seems different. Just don't rush into anything crazy, Pat. Don't let your romantic-comedy brain override your common sense."

Eli had already mapped his Shakespearean trajectory, complete with projected West End dates and potential Oscar nominations. "First the summer program, then the Master's, then the West End. And I will be your long-suffering, loyal best friend who occasionally directs your indie passion projects and writes your acceptance speeches." He clasped Patrick's hand. "Go forth and conquer. And don't forget your loyal subjects back in the colonies. We'll be watching. And judging. With cocktails."

He left New York on a wave of unfiltered euphoria. The flight felt like a dream, above the clouds, heading toward a future so bright it practically shimmered. He replayed moments with Victor, imagined London adventures and with a nervous flutter, refreshed his Shakespeare monologues. Everything finally felt in place: ambition and romance in harmony.

He landed at Heathrow with a bounce, the crisp London air a welcome change from humid New York. The terminal hummed with a different kind of energy than JFK, subdued yet purposeful, distinctly British.

He hailed a black cab, the iconic vehicle gleaming beneath the overcast sky like a cinematic prop. The driver, jovial and thick-accented, called, "Alright…where to?" Patrick gave the address of the St. Pancras Renaissance Hotel, thrilled by the grand name, Victorian splendor, and whispered secrets.

"Do you mind taking the scenic route?" he asked, leaning forward. "I'd love to see some of the spots. The real London, not just the airport highway."

"Right, then—scenic it is," the driver chuckled. "Most tourists just want to get there quick. But London, she's a lady who likes to be admired."

With a confident swerve, they plunged into the city. The generic outskirts of Heathrow softened into the London he had only seen in films and books. Double-deckers, impossibly red and tall, lumbered past with upper decks pressed with curious faces. Red phone booths stood like sentinels of a bygone era, vibrant splashes against muted brickwork. Elegant rows of terraced houses, their brick facades softened by time and ivy, whispered stories of generations.

They zipped past Hyde Park, a vast green rival to Central Park, and he pictured jogging its leafy paths, stumbling upon a tea garden or some hidden statue. Crossing the Thames, the murky, storied river mirrored a sky already tilting toward dusk, bruised purple and soft gray. He caught a glimpse of the Houses of Parliament, Big Ben steady, its clock face familiar and comforting, a calm guardian of the city. Each landmark felt like a postcard materializing, proof of a long-held dream.

The St. Pancras Renaissance rose from the streetscape like a Gothic cathedral, red brick and spires reaching skyward, a breathtaking testament to Victorian architecture. It looked less like a hotel and more like a monument, opulence and hushed grandeur. Patrick wanted to treat himself to one last night of luxury before student housing, an indulgence before communal bathrooms and questionable cafeteria food.

Checking in felt like stepping into another century. The lobby's soaring arches, stained glass, and polished marble amplified hushed voices and the delicate clink of china. His room matched the mood: high ceilings, ornate plasterwork, and a massive window over King's Cross Station where trains and commuters performed a daily ballet. He unpacked his small carry-on. His few possessions looked comically out of place, like a vagabond had broken into a palace. He placed his toothbrush next to a crystal water glass. It looked intimidated.

His bags barely grazed the floor before he pulled out his phone. Fingers trembling with excitement and nerves, he texted Victor: *Hey! Just landed and checked into the hotel. Let me know when you're free to meet up for the movie!*

He added an exclamation point. Then deleted it. Then added it back. Then added a second one. He hit send before he could add a third and look like a golden retriever on amphetamines.

He settled in, unpacked a few essentials, and admired the room's architecture. An hour passed. No reply. He told himself Victor was busy. Classes. Exploring. Saving orphans from a burning building. He was probably doing something heroic, which was why he couldn't text back.

Three hours in, the quiet was deafening. What had felt grand now felt cavernous. The Victorian Gothic décor started to feel less "romantic" and more "Dickensian orphanage."

Patrick paced the plush carpet. He checked his phone to make sure he had service. He turned airplane mode on and off. He briefly considered calling the front desk to ask if there was a city-wide signal outage affecting only extremely handsome men.

He stared at the window. *If he's dead, I'll be devastated,* Patrick thought. *If he's ignoring me, I will burn this hotel to the ground.*

At last, nearly five hours after the first text, his phone buzzed. Relief flared, then dimmed as his eyes moved over the message:

Victor: *Hey Patrick, I'm really sorry but we can't do this anymore. I wanted to be honest with you. I actually have a girlfriend, and I should have told you sooner. I was seeing her the entire time I was with you. Really sorry to have led you on. I do wish you the best and good luck this summer.*

Patrick stared at the screen.

A girlfriend.

The whole time.

He didn't cry immediately. He just felt a sharp, clarifying thud in his chest.

He read it again.

"I do wish you the best."

He let out a short, dry laugh.

The professionalism of it. It was breathtaking.

He dropped the phone on the bed.

Of course he had a girlfriend. It made perfect sense. The scarcity of dates. The unreturned calls. Patrick hadn't been a boyfriend; he'd been a side project. A hobby.

Fuck. Fuck him.

He looked around the room. The expensive wallpaper,

the heavy curtains, the crisp sheets. He had staged this whole evening for a romantic reunion, and now he was just a guy in an overpriced room with a suitcase full of hope and no one to give it to.

Then he remembered what was in his bag.

He walked over to his suitcase and pulled out the velvet pouch. Inside lay the two matching compass necklaces.

He stared at them.

"I bought matching jewelry," he whispered. "I should be put on a watchlist."

They weren't romantic anymore. They were evidence. They were small, silver monuments to his own delusion. He dropped the pouch back into the bag, burying it deep under his socks.

The tears came then, but they were angry tears. Hot and humiliating.

Was he destined for an endless parade of romantic misfires? Was something fundamentally wrong with him, something that drew these situations, these people who would lead him on and vanish, leaving only the bitter taste of regret?

He sat on the edge of the bed and looked at himself in the ornate mirror. Red eyes. Pale face.

"Wow. Stunning," he muttered to the reflection. "Thriving."

He needed a drink.

He washed his face, put on his shoes, and walked down

the elegant corridors. He refused to look sad. He channeled every ounce of his acting training into looking like a mysterious, wealthy traveler who *chose* to drink alone, rather than a man who had just been dumped via corporate memo.

The hotel bar was dimly lit. Expensive.

He climbed onto a velvet stool. The bartender drifted over.

"What can I get you?"

"Gin," Patrick said. "And tonic. But mostly gin."

He looked out the window at the lights of King's Cross. London. His dream city.

He was here. He was alone. And he was currently paying eighteen pounds for a drink to numb the fact that he was an idiot.

He wondered if Hamlet ever felt this spectacularly screwed. Probably. But Hamlet had the decency to die at the end. Patrick just had to wake up tomorrow and find a Pret A Manger.

CHAPTER 5

The morning light over St. Pancras cut sharp through the tall windows, gilding the carved arches and red-brick grandeur in an almost accusatory way. The day before, the place had felt like the gateway to his future, a palace where he could tuck away every ache of homesickness and imagine himself as one of the dreamers who belonged here.

But now it looked different, just as beautiful but with a kind of cruel detachment, as though it knew he had been discarded overnight and would not bother to disguise its indifference.

Patrick woke slowly, his body heavy with a kind of exhaustion that was not purely physical. His eyes were swollen, rimmed red, and for a long time he simply lay still, staring at the ceiling's intricate plasterwork. The pattern seemed endless, looping scrolls and flourishes etched in cream, a frozen celebration of permanence.

Permanence, he thought bitterly. The opposite of

Victor's blunt, six-word message that still pulsed like a brand on the back of his eyelids: *"We can't do this anymore."*

When he finally moved, it was with the heaviness of someone dragging himself through wet cement. The ornate mirror across the room showed a man he barely recognized, face pale, puffy, his lips chapped, hair a chaotic mess. He looked like one of those doomed Antarctic explorers, except instead of frostbite, he had puffy eyes and unprocessed gay trauma.

Good morning, London. Here's your tragic leading man.

The bathroom, so luxurious previously with its gold fittings and endless hot water, now felt like a sterile museum. He splashed his face repeatedly, as if the water might dissolve the ache lodged behind his ribs. His reflection did not improve, but at least the sting on his skin made him feel alive.

Dressing required little thought. Jeans, a loose shirt, something that would not betray the storm inside. He shoved his belongings into his suitcase, no longer caring about the neatness he usually obsessed over. Even the concierge's smile seemed to whisper, "Ah, yes, another boy who cried in Room 314."

Outside, the city was already awake, its bustle both exhilarating and merciless. Patrick hailed a black cab, his voice flat as he gave the driver the address for Schaffer House, RADA's student housing. No detours, no scenic drives. He wanted distance between himself and the grand hotel that had so quickly transformed from dream to mausoleum.

Schaffer House, when they pulled up, could not have been more different. It was plain, a little tired, its brickwork softened by decades of London weather. But there was comfort in its humility. Countless students had carried their own heartbreaks, their own ambitions. The walls seemed to hum faintly with all those past lives, storing both failures and triumphs in equal measure.

His new room was bare: a narrow bed, a desk scarred with old etchings, a wardrobe that creaked on its hinges. Compared to the opulence of last night, it looked almost monastic. Yet there was relief in that simplicity.

He threw open the window, letting in a breath of thick summer air that carried with it the faint aroma of brick dust and diesel. London's humidity wrapped him close, sticky and immediate.

Patrick unpacked methodically, each shirt folded into the wardrobe as if burying fragments of the night before. At the bottom of the suitcase, he found the velvet pouch with the compass necklaces. For a moment his chest clenched. He considered tossing it into the desk drawer and forgetting it, but instead he left it on the windowsill where the light caught the silver. A reminder, not of Victor but of his own need to keep moving forward.

By the time his suitcase lay empty, his chest felt lighter, if only because the act of unpacking resembled commitment. He was here. This was real.

Still, silence pressed on him, and silence was dangerous. He needed to move. He needed RADA.

He grabbed his orientation folder, its weight disproportionate to the few papers it contained, and set out on foot toward Gower Street. London looked different now that he was no longer shielded by a taxi's glass.

The streets breathed intimacy: bookshops spilling their wares onto crooked tables, pubs leaking laughter that trailed after him, a scatter of art galleries punctuating the brickwork with bold posters.

When he reached the corner where RADA stood, Patrick's breath caught. The building was modest in comparison to its neighbors, but its energy radiated outward. Two sculptures flanked the entrance, figures frozen in the midst of performance, guardians of art who dared you to falter.

It was a bit dramatic, Patrick admitted to himself, but then again, drama was exactly why he was here.

He paused, letting his gaze meet theirs, and felt the spark return, faint but real.

Crossing the threshold was like slipping through a membrane. The air was different here, charged with invisible echoes of every voice that had rehearsed on these floors, every career that had begun with trembling hands on these door handles.

Photographs of alumni lined the walls, their gazes

stern, measuring. Patrick's stomach fluttered, half nerves, half reverence.

In the common room, students gathered, their chatter filling the space with a patchwork of accents. The energy was nervous, expectant, like the collective inhale before a curtain rises.

Patrick drew on the performer's smile he had honed over years, charming, approachable, masking the bruise of heartbreak.

At the sign-in table, staff divided them into five groups: Fortune, Swan, Lysander, Rose, and Perdita. His group was Fortune, which felt like either a blessing or a curse depending on how you spun it.

He noted the variety of ages in the room, some barely out of college, others clearly in their forties or fifties. Theater, at least, respected no age limits.

He entered the smaller classroom assigned to Fortune. Being among the first was unnerving—no background noise to blend into but also a chance to establish himself. He chose a seat by the window, posture open but casual, a balancing act between interest and aloofness.

The door opened, and a woman stepped in with the kind of energy that filled corners. Short bob haircut, eyes that sparkled with mischief, and a smile so immediate it felt like sunshine breaking through.

"Hi! I'm Jessica—Jess," she said, extending her hand.

She was sun-soaked and stunning. Stylish brown hair

tumbled in bouncing curls around a face that was soft and inviting, though her eyes were framed by eyeliner so razor-sharp it looked like it could cut glass.

"Patrick." His handshake was steady, and hers was firm, grounding.

"Where you from?" Her voice carried a West Coast lilt, melodic and inviting.

"New York. You?"

"L.A., born and raised. Did some TV back home"—she waved a hand dismissively—"but I wanted real training. You can only play the 'sassy neighbor' so many times before you want to scream."

Patrick laughed, sensing a kindred spirit. She had the vibe of a cynic with a heart of gold, armed with a tongue as sharp as her makeup.

The door didn't just open; it was assaulted.

In stormed a man who seemed to be vibrating at a different frequency than the rest of the planet. He sucked the oxygen out of the room instantly.

He wore a University of Florida sweatshirt, expensive designer athletic wear that had clearly never seen a gym, and hair so rigid with gel it could probably withstand a hurricane. But it was the teeth that caught Patrick off guard—veneers that were just a shade too white, gleaming with aggressive prosperity.

"Heyyy!" he bellowed, volume level at a solid ten. "This the Fortune group? Amazing. I'm Jacob."

He didn't wait for a response. He dropped an expensive leather bag onto the floor with a heavy thud.

"Just wrapped a killer *Midsummer Night's Dream*—did three roles. Long story. It was insane, total tour de force," Jacob continued, scanning the room as if checking for a camera crew. "My parents are in the industry. Producers. You probably haven't heard of their stuff unless you watch movies at 3 AM on a Tuesday, but hey, streaming pays the bills, right? They just donated for the new tech wing renovation here. So, boom. Here I am."

No one had asked.

He dropped into a chair and immediately launched into a blow-by-blow of his theatrical résumé, complete with accents and hand gestures.

Patrick exchanged a glance with Jess that said, "We are absolutely in hell."

In Patrick's mental filing cabinet, Jacob went under "Florida Man."

The next arrival was almost cinematic in contrast.

She stepped in like she'd been lit by a key light, dark, glossy hair cascading over her shoulders, her features elegant and highlighted by classic makeup and a bold red lip. She wore a tailored black blazer and wide-leg trousers, the look crisp, unfussy, and radiating Old-Hollywood cool.

She looked like Elizabeth Taylor had decided to audit a drama class.

Patrick straightened slightly as she passed. "Hi, I'm

Patrick," he said, offering a tentative smile.

She turned to him, her expression soft but unreadable. "Hello," she said. "I'm Olivia."

Her voice was low and melodic like the first few bars of a jazz record. She took a seat two rows ahead with quiet grace, crossed her legs, and looked around the room with calm interest.

There was nothing haughty about her; it was as if she simply didn't need to try.

Patrick found himself a little in awe. She hadn't said much, but somehow she'd already entered with more presence than Jacob's entire résumé.

More students trickled in, nervous laughter filling the air. Patrick felt the stir of belonging, faint but rising. He was part of something now, a constellation of dreamers, each carrying their own invisible baggage. It was all a bit batshit, really. An international heartbreak escape turned drama school fever dream. But sure. Normal Tuesday.

The room shifted when the door opened again. A man entered, lean and wiry, his presence filling the air before he even spoke. Mid-forties, his hair a little unruly, clothes simple but purposeful, he looked like he had stepped straight off a rehearsal floor rather than from an office. There was a tension to him, a hum, as if his very skin conducted electricity.

He did not introduce himself immediately. Instead he let the silence lengthen, studying each face as though taking their measure.

When he finally spoke, his voice cracked like a whip, resonant and textured, the kind of voice that carried without needing volume.

"Hello, Fortune. Repeat after me: Blow, winds, and crack your cheeks!"

The line thundered through the room. Some students echoed it timidly, voices cracking, laughter bubbling at the edges. The man cut them off with a flick of his hand.

"Again. With breath. With fury."

This time the group tried harder, their voices rough but louder. He pressed them once more, gesturing with his arms as though conducting an orchestra.

Patrick felt his chest expand, breath surging, and when the words came out, they seemed to rip something loose inside him. The line roared from twenty mouths at once, layered and chaotic.

If his mother could see him screaming at a wall right now, Patrick thought, she'd finally have him committed.

The man underscored their voices with his own rumbling growl, mimicking thunder, slapping his hands against the desk for percussion. Suddenly the room was a storm. Students leaned forward, caught in the swell, until he silenced them with nothing more than a lifted palm.

The quiet that followed was charged, as though lightning still lingered in the air.

The man nodded once. "*King Lear*, Act III, Scene 2,"

he said simply, then allowed a smile to break across his face. "I'm Garrett. Your instructor. This summer, we'll journey through Shakespeare together. It will be glorious. It will be terrifying. And it will demand more from you than you think you can give."

Garrett began calling roll.

"Jacob?"

"Here!" Jacob boomed, his arm shooting up. "Ready to work!"

"Jessica?"

"Present," Jess replied with a grin.

"Patrick?"

Patrick lifted a hand, his voice steady.

"Olivia?"

A quiet "yes" from the corner.

Then Garrett's eyes scanned the page again. "Dean?"

Silence. The pause stretched. Garrett tilted his head, then made a note on his clipboard without comment.

He handed out schedules, each sheet packed from dawn 'til dusk: voice warm-ups, movement classes, scene study, lectures, daily rehearsals. The sheer density made Patrick's pulse quicken. This was not just a summer program; it was boot camp.

"You will sweat. You will falter," Garrett said, pacing before them. "And if you are lucky, you will fail spectacularly. Because only in failure do you meet your limits. And only by meeting them do you break through."

Patrick scribbled notes he did not need to, his pen nearly tearing the page. He already felt the stirrings of something inside him, an ache to be tested.

Then Garrett paused, his voice softening, conspiratorial. "This year, for the first time, the program mounts a full Shakespeare production. A complete staging. All twenty-five students from all groups will audition."

The words dropped like a stone into water, ripples spreading instantly. Heads turned; whispers cascaded around the room. Some students straightened in excitement, others visibly tensed. Patrick felt his heart leap.

"Now, about the casting," Garrett said, clasping his hands behind his back. "We are approaching this with a non-traditional lens. We cast based on the soul. Anyone can play any part. We strip away the expectations to find the truth."

Patrick nodded along, though a small, terrified voice in the back of his head whispered, Please, God, don't let me be the Nurse.

Garrett stopped pacing and looked at them, a mischievous glint in his eye.

"Which is why," he announced, "we will be mounting *Romeo and Juliet.*"

A collective exhale, a mix of relief and recognition. A safe choice.

But Garrett wasn't finished. His smile widened, slyly.

"With a twist," he added, his voice dropping to a conspiratorial whisper. "Since we are casting entirely on spirit, and since the chemistry in the auditions will dictate the roles...you should prepare for any eventuality. We will let the text and your chemistry decide."

The room stilled.

For a moment, silence hung heavy. Then it broke in a flurry—surprised laughter, gasps, the rustle of possibility.

Patrick's chest surged as though someone had struck a match inside it. He barely registered Jess's delighted squeal beside him or Jacob's muttered, "Well, that's different." What he felt was an almost painful rush of possibility. Heartbreak, rejection, last night's text—they blurred, dimmed, eclipsed by this horizon opening in front of him.

Patrick swallowed hard, steadying himself. He wanted it. He wanted it more than anything. And for the first time since arriving in London, the ache of Victor's absence no longer defined him.

The dream was here, alive, and it was demanding his whole heart.

CHAPTER 6

With Garrett's schedule in hand, a densely packed itinerary that looked less like a summer program and more like a theatrical boot camp, Patrick joined the gentle flow of students navigating the intricate network of corridors. But the initial awe of the alumni photos and the hushed reverence of the main hall suddenly curdled into something else: intimidation.

Every turning seemed to lead to another, every doorway hinting at a hidden studio or a dusty archive. He passed rooms where muffled piano notes escaped, others where voices boomed with Shakespearean verse, and still others where the rhythmic thud of tap shoes echoed.

A minute ago, it had sounded like a symphony. Now, it just sounded like noise.

The ache of Victor's absence, which had been momentarily eclipsed by the casting news, came rushing back with a vengeance. It was a physical blow, a tightness in his chest that made it hard to breathe. What was he doing here?

He stopped in the middle of the hallway, ignoring the students streaming past him. He looked at a glowing green exit sign.

It would be so easy. He could turn around. He could walk out the front entrance, hail a black cab, go back to the hotel, pack his bag, and be at Heathrow by noon. He could go home.

The temptation was so strong it made his knees weak. Just leave. Just bail. Stop trying to be the tragic hero and just be the sad ex-boyfriend in his own bed.

Patrick took a deep, shaky breath. He gripped the strap of his bag until his knuckles turned white.

No, he told himself. *You are already here. Just get through the first day. Just get through the next hour.*

He forced his feet to move.

His first class was Voice and Speech, held in a large, airy studio. He paused at the door, his hand hovering over the handle. He pushed the door open.

It was lined with mirrors, reflecting the nervous energy of the incoming students, and smelled faintly of old wood, determination, and perhaps a hint of decades of expelled breath.

Their teacher Diana was indeed as described: a quirky but amazing woman with a wild mane of silver hair that seemed to defy gravity and all known styling products. Her eyes twinkled with mischievous intelligence, hinting at a deep well of wisdom and a playful spirit. She wore vibrant, flowing clothes that billowed around her as she moved with an almost ethereal grace, despite her age, like a benevolent, slightly unhinged theatrical fairy godmother.

"Alright, darlings, welcome!" Diana boomed, her voice surprisingly powerful for her slight frame, filling the room with a warmth that cut through the last vestiges of Patrick's emotional chill.

"Voice is breath, breath is life! And life, my little darlings, is all about connection! To yourselves, to the text, to each other! So, for our very first exercise, I want you all to find a partner. Someone near you! And quickly now— no dawdling! Let's get those connections flowing, get that energy circulating!"

Her gaze swept over the room, a silent command for immediate action.

The room erupted into a flurry of motion, chairs scraping, voices murmuring as students scattered to pair up. Patrick found himself standing awkwardly in the middle of the room, still feeling shell-shocked by the newness, unsure who to approach. His internal monologue, usually a witty stream of consciousness, had momentarily short-circuited, leaving him with nothing but a frantic, silent hum.

Jacob suddenly appeared at his elbow, eyes darting everywhere at once. "Patrick, right? You don't have a partner yet, do you? I heard there's a TV actor in this program—maybe British, maybe American. If I spot him, I'm locking that down, buddy. No offense."

Before Patrick could answer, Jacob had already zipped away toward another corner, leaving only a trail of speculation behind.

Buddy. There was nothing Patrick hated more than being called bud or buddy. Definitely a strike against Jacob in the mental file he was already keeping.

Patrick sighed. Every class needs a Jacob. Gossip travels faster than a Florida Man headline.

He told himself to just pick someone, anyone. This wasn't a dating app; it was a voice class. No pressure. Just pick a human.

Just as he was contemplating the social etiquette of politely kidnapping a partner or perhaps simply dissolving into a puddle of existential dread and becoming one with the dusty floorboards, the door to the studio opened with a soft click.

To the rest of the room, nothing changed. Diana was still shouting instructions about diaphragms; Jacob was still loudly talking about himself across the room. The chaos of students shuffling for space continued uninterrupted.

But for Patrick, everything just…stopped.

It wasn't that the sound cut out. It was that his brain simply stopped processing it. The chatter, the footsteps, the scraping chairs—it all receded into a dull, gray hum, pushed to the very edges of his consciousness.

The world narrowed down to a single focal point: the open door.

A man sauntered in, a little late, a whirlwind of cool nonchalance that somehow made the entire room seem to tilt on its axis, as if the very air rearranged itself around him.

Oh. Well, fuck me, Patrick thought.

The universe really had a flair for dramatic irony.

Ten minutes into drama school, and he was already in a scene from a gay Jane Austen adaptation.

Patrick's eyes, still red-rimmed from crying, widened. He was truly taken aback by how beautiful this man was. He was a breathtaking, impossible blend of every beautiful guy Patrick had ever seen in magazines, films, or on TV rolled into one impossibly captivating package.

His dark-brown hair, perfectly disheveled, fell casually over his forehead with that one perfect piece hanging down over his eye, giving him an air of effortless coolness and quiet mystery. His jawline was sharp, sculpted, a perfect line that made Patrick's breath catch. His lips, full and subtly curved, held a hint of a smile, as if he knew a secret joke the rest of the world wasn't privy to.

He wore a classic white t-shirt, its fabric soft and worn, emblazoned with the iconic black Beatles logo, and over it, a leather jacket that looked like it had seen countless adventures and probably smelled faintly of rebellious spirit and expensive coffee.

He was, quite simply, the perfect man. Or at least, the perfect distraction from the crushing reality of his recent past, a beacon of unexpected beauty in his personal storm.

Patrick felt a familiar, unwelcome pull, a gravitational force he'd spent the last day trying to escape, a magnetic tug that defied all his carefully constructed defenses.

He knew it was too soon. Way too soon. He had just gotten burned. Badly.

He had to spend a whole summer with these people. He told himself to be good. Just be friends. Just professional colleagues. Nothing more.

He repeated the mantra in his head, a desperate plea for self-control: *Be good, Patrick. For the love of all that is holy, just be good.*

"Ah, you must be Dean!" Diana said, a warm smile on her face, completely unfazed by his tardiness. Her voice snapped the world back into motion. The ambient noise of the room rushed back in like a flood, leaving Patrick blinking, disoriented, as if waking from a trance. "Welcome, welcome! Just in time for our first pairing exercise. Find a partner, love. And jacket off, please. Let's get you ready to breathe freely."

Dean nodded, a soft smile playing on his lips, and with a fluid movement, he shrugged off the leather jacket, revealing a perfectly toned, lean, athletic build that moved with an easy grace.

He was just a little taller than Patrick, a comfortable

height difference that Patrick, in his current state of emotional vulnerability, instinctively appreciated. He was the kind of tall that felt protective, not towering. A comforting presence.

Patrick found his gaze lingering on Dean's strong forearms, the subtle ripple of muscle as he folded his jacket, and quickly averted his eyes, a blush creeping up his neck.

Dean turned to face Patrick, his eyes a captivating shade of hazel. "Hello," he said, his voice a low, melodic rumble laced with the most soothing British accent Patrick had ever heard.

And there it was. The first proper British voice he'd heard from a fellow student since arriving.

It was like warm honey on a cold day, a balm to his bruised soul.

"Hello," Patrick managed, "I'm Patrick."

"Alright, you two! Perfect!" Diana clapped her hands together, oblivious to the subtle, electric current now humming between them, a conductor of human connection, a silent orchestrator of growing chemistry.

Patrick's brain, which had just spent the last twenty-four hours in a self-pitying tailspin, struggled to process the instructions. He looked at Dean, who gave him an encouraging smile, a silent invitation to trust, a gentle reassurance that everything would be alright.

"You go first," Dean offered, his accent making even

that simple phrase sound like a poetic invitation, a whispered promise of something intriguing, something new.

Patrick nodded, trying to calm his racing heart, which was currently doing a frantic tap dance in his chest. He bent forward, hands reaching for his toes, his body feeling oddly stiff, a physical manifestation of his emotional armor.

He closed his eyes, focusing on Diana's instructions. He felt Dean's hands gently rest at the base of his spine. A warm current, surprisingly pleasant, spread through him, chasing away a sliver of the lingering chill, a tiny spark of warmth in the cold grip of his anxiety.

"Alright," Diana chimed in. "Now, one vertebra at a time. Imagine it stacking. And a little pillow of air in between. Feel the space opening up, feel the release."

Dean's fingers, strong yet incredibly gentle, began their slow ascent. Patrick felt each vertebra, one by one, being "stacked" as he slowly, almost imperceptibly, began to rise. It was an incredibly intimate exercise, one that forced a level of trust and physical awareness Patrick hadn't anticipated.

He focused on his breathing, trying to make it diaphragmatic, trying to ignore the sudden, undeniable thrill that was starting to course through him, a jolt of pure, unadulterated excitement. His body, usually so attuned to movement, was now acutely aware of every subtle shift, every warm touch, every brush of Dean's fingers against his skin.

His breathing, however, was starting to get a little less diaphragmatic and a lot more excited. Here he was, in his first RADA class, ten minutes in, and he was being touched by the most beautiful guy in the entire room.

He was a giggling, internally screaming mess, a walking theatrical disaster. He reminded himself to calm down. It was too soon. He had to be good. Just friends. Professional. *Focus, Patrick, for God's sake, focus!*

"Another vertebra," Dean whispered, his fingers moving higher, "pillow of air. Almost there."

Dean's fingers reached the top of Patrick's spine. Patrick slowly straightened, his head the last thing to come up. He opened his eyes, and Dean was standing there.

"Did that feel alright?" Dean said with a smile.

Patrick, still slightly dazed, managed to nod. "Yeah, yes it did," he said, the words tumbling out a little too eagerly, a little too breathless. Then, realizing how weird that sounded, he quickly added, "You have incredibly strong hands. I mean, my back felt...very responsive. Quite a release, actually. My spine feels...very present. Very...worked on."

Had he always talked like a Victorian ghost in heat? Apparently, yes.

Dean tilted his head slightly. "You have a lot of knots in your back."

Patrick blinked. "Yeah. Probably because of being a

dancer."

Dean's smile deepened. "Oh, nice! Makes sense. My mum says my posture's too stiff."

"Alright, darlings, switch!" Diana yelled, her voice cutting through the intimate bubble they had inadvertently created, a welcome if jarring interruption, like a stage manager calling "places!"

Patrick and Dean swapped places. Patrick felt a tremor of nerves but also a surge of excitement.

As Dean bent over, reaching for his toes, Diana's voice boomed again. "Now, before you begin, I want the standing partner to gently massage the low back of your partner. Just to get the blood flowing, the air moving! Feel the connection, feel the release! Let your hands be extensions of your intention, darlings!"

Patrick's eyes widened. Massaging his low back?

He swallowed hard. His palms were suddenly damp, his stomach staging a full-blown coup, butterflies armed with tiny knives.

Was the universe trying to fucking kill him?

Ten minutes into drama school, and he was already one vertebra away from a gay meltdown. Of course. Of course, this was happening.

He glanced at Diana, who looked absolutely delighted about the spiritual intimacy of lumbar massage, like this was just another Tuesday in her barefoot fairy godmother life.

He placed his hands on either side of Dean's waist, just above his hips, and gently began to rub.

Dean's skin was warm, impossibly smooth beneath his fingertips, and the lean muscles beneath felt supple and exquisitely strong, a testament to a body that clearly knew its way around a stage, a gym, or both.

Patrick felt a distinct, undeniable thrill ripple through him, a jolt that had nothing to do with professional curiosity and everything to do with the unexpected, electric intimacy of the moment.

He focused on the sensation, the radiating warmth, the subtle shifting of Dean's body under his hands, trying desperately to ignore the way his own heart was now doing a full-blown Broadway number, a frantic, desperate rhythm against his ribs.

The scent of Dean, clean and woodsy, filled his nostrils, a dizzying, intoxicating aroma that made his head spin, a scent he knew he wouldn't soon forget.

And then Patrick started to giggle. It started as a small, internal tremor, then bubbled up, escaping his lips, a soft, involuntary sound like a burst of unexpected sunshine, a release of nervous energy.

Dean straightened slightly, opening his eyes, a surprised smile on his face, a hint of amusement playing in his hazel depths.

"That feels great," Dean said as his smile widened, a crinkling at the corners of his eyes that made them sparkle, a genuine, uninhibited grin.

They continued the exercise, Dean slowly rising under Patrick's touch, each vertebra, each "pillow of air." By the time Dean was standing upright, Patrick felt a lightness he hadn't experienced since before his current arrival in London.

This man, this Dean, had a warmth, an ease about him that was incredibly disarming, a genuine kindness that cut through all of Patrick's carefully constructed defenses, dismantling his walls brick by gentle brick.

There was an instant connection, a spark that wasn't necessarily romantic but undeniably there, a shared frequency that resonated between them, a quiet hum of recognition.

Patrick was amazed at how perfect this man seemed. Too perfect, perhaps. He found himself staring again at the slope of Dean's neck, the way his smile unfolded slowly, deliberately. He looked away before anyone could notice.

He needed to take it slow. He didn't even know if Dean was gay or if he had a secret girlfriend or some other hidden quirk.

He repeated his mantra: Just friends. *Be good. You have to spend a whole summer with these people. Don't screw this up. Don't fall too fast.*

After class, Patrick quickly gathered his things, his heart still thrumming in his chest. He wanted to talk to Dean. He needed to talk to Dean.

He turned, ready to approach him, but a wall of University of Florida merchandise blocked his path.

"Dean, right? You've got a look, man," Jacob was already there, cornering Dean by the mirrors, looming over him with aggressive enthusiasm. "Seriously. Very marketable. We should grab a drink. My parents are producers."

Dean looked polite but slightly cornered, clutching his leather jacket like a shield. "Oh, er, right. That's... very kind."

Patrick froze. He should just walk away. It was safer. Jacob was loud, Dean was out of his league, and Patrick was a fragile, heartbroken mess who had cried in a hotel room less than twenty-four hours ago.

Don't do it, his brain warned. *Do not engage. Go back to your room, eat a sandwich, and protect your peace.*

But then he saw Dean's eyes flicker over Jacob's shoulder, meeting his. There was a faint, desperate plea in them.

Patrick made a choice.

"Hey, Dean?" Patrick stepped around Jacob, forcing a casual confidence he absolutely did not feel. "Sorry to interrupt. I think you might have left your water bottle by the mats?"

It was a lie—Dean was holding his water bottle—but it was enough to break Jacob's rhythm.

Jacob huffed, looking annoyed at the intrusion. "We're

talking strategy, Patrick. Networking."

"Right—huge stuff," Patrick said, breezing past the comment. He turned his focus entirely to Dean, ignoring the glare burning into the side of his head. "Actually, while I have you, I was wondering if you knew the area well? I'm looking for a movie theater… or, uh, a cinema near here?"

Jacob rolled his eyes. "A movie theater? You're in London, dude. We're going to the pub."

"It's a screening of *Empire Strikes Back*," Patrick said, leaning into the nerdiness, knowing it was the perfect Jacob-repellent.

"*Star Wars*? Seriously?" Jacob scoffed, checking his watch as if he had suddenly remembered he was too cool for this conversation. "Right. Well. I'm gonna go find the others. Have fun with the space wizards. Dean, catch you later."

Jacob grabbed his bag and stormed out, effectively bored into submission.

The silence that followed was instant and blissful.

Dean let out a long, relieved exhale, his shoulders dropping two inches.

"Cheers for that," Dean said, a genuine smile breaking through.

Patrick's throat went dry. The obstacle was gone. Now it was just him, the most beautiful man in London, and a terrible idea.

Say something stupid, he prayed. *Ask him about the weather.*

Ask him where the bathroom is.

Instead, his mouth betrayed him.

"I wasn't lying about the movie, by the way," Patrick said, his voice slightly higher than he intended. "I do have tickets for *Empire* tonight. And my friend bailed."

He paused, bracing himself. "Would you want to go?"

The silence stretched for a heartbeat. In that second, Patrick prepared his exit strategy. He prepared to be laughed at, to be politely rejected, to be told he was barking up the wrong tree.

Then, Dean's eyes lit up.

"*Empire Strikes Back*? I'd love to. That sounds brilliant, mate."

They exchanged numbers. Their fingers brushed.

"I'll text you the details," Patrick said.

"Sounds good," Dean replied.

Patrick watched him walk out.

Patrick stood alone in the studio, a small, triumphant smile spreading across his face.

He had no idea what the night would hold. But for the first time since landing in London, Patrick felt a flicker of hope.

But as he looked down at the new contact in his phone, the word echoed in his head.

Mate.

Brilliant, *mate.*

Patrick let out a long breath, thinking back to the hallway an hour ago. If he had given in, he would be at Heathrow right now.

Instead, he was here. Terrified, yes. Confused, definitely.

But as he looked at Dean's name on the screen.

Patrick sighed.

It felt like fortune. Or possibly a beautifully lit disaster in the making.

CHAPTER 7

The cinema on Portobello Road was the kind of charmingly worn-in place Patrick secretly adored but wouldn't admit to back in New York. Unlike the gleaming, soulless boxes in Times Square, this one had mismatched velvet seats that creaked gently and a popcorn machine that looked like it had survived two world wars.

He stood out front, pretending to check his phone, trying not to look like he was waiting. Which, of course, he very much was. For Dean. Who he wasn't calling a date. Not out loud. Not even internally. Absolutely not.

Still, he had changed shirts three times. And applied cologne. Twice. Which he was now regretting because he smelled like vaguely like a department store explosion.

When Dean appeared, strolling toward him like a film student who hadn't yet realized he was the main character, Patrick had to take a discreet breath. Dean looked unfairly good in a navy sweater, sleeves pushed to the elbows, curls still damp from the evening air like he'd walked through a very flattering cloud.

"You're early," Dean said, flashing that grin that made it hard to think in complete sentences.

"I'm American," Patrick replied, slipping his phone into his jacket and finally uncrossing his legs so he could stand like a human being. "It's a compulsion. We show up early and apologize too much."

Dean laughed, warm and easy. "Or maybe you just really wanted good seats."

Patrick smiled, heart doing its own choreography. Overhead, the battered marquee flickered weakly, offering up *Empire Strikes Back* and a local documentary with a title so vague it could've been anything from farming to existential dread. Still, it was the kind of theater that felt like it had stories in the walls, and Patrick already liked it.

Inside, a single, eccentric usher in a tweed jacket took their tickets with the gravitas of a priest receiving confessions. His glasses, perched precariously on his nose, glinted in the lobby's soft, flickering light. He had the faintest smirk, like he knew every secret ending.

"Right then, lads. Screen three. And try not to spoil the ending for anyone, alright?" he murmured, voice gravelly and conspiratorial.

Patrick was quickly falling for British understatement. Humor here came dry. Chilled martini dry.

"Wouldn't dream of it," Dean replied. "Wouldn't want to ruin Vader's big reveal. Imagine the collective gasp. The fainting spells. The mass hysteria."

He winked at the usher, who gave a faint, approving nod, clearly used to theater students and their flair.

"Spoilers," Patrick muttered, nudging Dean as they headed down the aisle. "You're a menace."

Their shoes squeaked against the worn carpet. The smell of stale popcorn and old velvet filled the air. Objectively questionable but somehow comforting. Dean's arm brushed his as they slid into the creaky seats, and Patrick felt it like a jolt.

Just static. Or nerves. Or maybe this was a date.

He was not going to interrogate it. It definitely wasn't the proximity to Dean that had Patrick's pulse skipping. His brain shoved that thought into a box marked Not Today, Satan.

Dean held up a bucket of popcorn the size of a carry-on suitcase. "Snack?"

"And I've got Maltesers," he added, producing a red packet like a magician. "A classic. Absolutely essential to the full British cinema experience."

Patrick peered into the popcorn, then eyed the Maltesers like he was choosing a Pokémon starter. "Oh, definitely Maltesers," he said, solemn. "But also a handful of whatever that is," he added, gesturing vaguely at the popcorn, trying to look chill while already halfway in. "I'm embracing the culture. Method snacking. Very RADA."

Dean chuckled, low and warm, the sound vibrating

through Patrick's seat and ribcage and spine.

"A bold move," Dean said. "Our sweets tend to whisper rather than scream. Not like your Sour Patch creations."

Patrick popped a Malteser into his mouth. Crunchy, light, chocolatey. A charming surprise. "Honestly? Subtle is a nice change. My emotional taste buds have been through it lately."

Dean gave him a look but didn't press.

"Speaking of sweets," Patrick said, needing something safer, "what was your childhood favorite? Like, the one you'd push a toddler for. No judgment."

Dean tilted his head, considering. "Wonka Bars. The ones with the popping candy inside. Discontinued, of course. A tragedy."

"A confectionery tragedy," Patrick agreed. "History will remember."

"But you know what never goes out of style?" Patrick continued. "Watermelon Sour Patch Kids. Perfection. First, it's tart, then it's like biting into neon joy. I will not be taking questions."

Dean blinked. "Are those legal?"

Patrick gasped. "Dean. Dean. That's your cultural homework now. I'm bringing you a bag, and we're going to change your life."

Dean grinned, teeth flashing in the dim light.

The lights dimmed. The previews rolled.

And Patrick felt the strange, giddy weightlessness of being exactly where he wanted to be.

But then came the armrest.

It was a shared armrest. A very narrow one. Patrick carefully kept his elbows tucked into his ribs like a T-Rex to avoid contact, but Dean, relaxed and expansive, let his arm rest naturally.

His elbow bumped Patrick's. Patrick twitched.

He froze. If he moved, it would make it weird. If he stayed, it was also weird. And why was Dean's arm so hot? Was the man running a fever, or was Patrick just hyper-fixating on a stranger's tricep like a Victorian spinster?

Dean shifted, settling in, and his forearm pressed firmly against Patrick's. He didn't pull away.

Patrick stopped breathing for a solid ten seconds.

The Lucasfilm logo shimmered across the screen. The opening crawl began its slow, iconic ascent.

Patrick felt something shift in his chest.

Not just nostalgia. Not just cinematic joy.

Something warmer. Quieter.

Dangerous, maybe.

They settled into that comfortable silence that only movie theaters allow, full of unspoken agreements, half-shared glances, and the occasional rustle of popcorn. Dean leaned back, his arm barely grazing Patrick's again, and Patrick didn't move. He pretended it didn't send another zip of static up his spine.

Throughout the film, they laughed quietly at C-3PO's dramatic flailing, gasped in unison during the asteroid field chase, and exchanged knowing looks at every memorable beat. Their shoulders brushed occasionally, each contact a quiet punctuation mark Patrick tried not to read into.

He told himself he was focused on the film. On the story.

But he found himself watching Dean more than the screen.

The way Dean leaned forward during tense scenes. The way his brow furrowed when Luke was trapped in the Wampa cave. The subtle chewing of his bottom lip when Han and Leia argued. That barely-there smile when Yoda made his cryptic quips.

Dean's joy was infectious. Earnest. Like someone seeing it all for the first time, even if he wasn't.

And when Vader delivered the iconic line "I am your father," Patrick glanced over and saw that Dean was already looking at him, that same wide-eyed spark lighting his face like a kid seeing fireworks.

It made the line feel new. Like Patrick was discovering it for the first time too.

The credits rolled. John Williams's score swelled. Patrick felt full and warm in a way that had nothing to do with popcorn.

They stretched and slowly made their way out of the theater, squinting against the reentry into fluorescent lobby light. The city outside was damp and cool, rain-slicked pavement glinting beneath the glow of streetlamps.

"That was brilliant," Dean said, pulling his jacket tighter. "Never gets old. Though I maintain Han should've just listened about the odds."

"Honestly," Patrick agreed, still a little dazed. "It hits every time. Even knowing what's coming, still gets me."

They walked slowly, letting the evening unfold around them. Portobello Road's charm hadn't faded with the night. The cobblestones shimmered faintly. Streetlights cast their golden hue over pastel buildings. The world felt hushed and cinematic, like the third act of a romcom that knew how to pace itself.

Patrick was so busy looking at the architecture and Dean's profile that he misjudged the curb and stumbled slightly.

Dean's hand shot out, catching Patrick's elbow to steady him. "Easy there, twinkle toes. Thought you were a dancer?"

"I am," Patrick said, face heating up instantly as he regained his balance. "This is...artistic falling. It's contemporary."

Dean laughed, but he didn't let go of Patrick's elbow immediately. His grip was warm through the fabric of Patrick's coat. He held it for a beat longer than necessary before dropping his hand.

Patrick's skin tingled where he had been touched.

Great. Now he was going to be thinking about an elbow grab for the next three business days.

Patrick inhaled deeply. The air smelled like stone and rain. London had a scent, and he was beginning to like it.

"So…RADA," Dean said, hands tucked in his pockets, voice casual but interested. "Still feeling the sparkle, or has the magic worn off under the weight of early morning breathing exercises?"

Patrick laughed. "Oh, definitely both. The sparkle's still there, somewhere under the existential panic and my screaming diaphragm."

"Sounds like the true RADA experience."

"It's intense," Patrick admitted. "In a good way. Everyone's super talented. Focused. Hungry. It's a lot to walk into, especially after—well—everything."

Dean glanced at him sideways. "You mean the...welcome committee heartbreak thing?"

Patrick smiled, tight-lipped. "Yeah. That."

A beat of quiet passed between them. Dean didn't push. Just walked alongside him, a grounding presence.

"It was exactly what I needed, though," Patrick said softly. "Tonight. This. It kind of...turned the day around."

Dean glanced over, that same soft smile in his eyes. "I'm glad. You seemed like you needed a good distraction."

They passed a pub spilling laughter into the street, the warmth of it brushing them in contrast to the night's chill. Patrick felt the edges of his worry start to loosen.

Dean asked, "So what's your story then? You mentioned Broadway?"

Patrick shrugged, a little bashful. "Yeah. Dancer. Ensemble. Some decent credits. Nothing major but enough to keep me fed and sore all the time."

"I bet it was amazing."

"It was," Patrick said, and he meant it. "Grueling. Rewarding. Eight shows a week, sometimes covering multiple tracks. Rehearsals during the day. Constant pressure to be perfect. But there's nothing like it. That feeling when you're mid-performance and everything just clicks."

Dean nodded, listening intently. Patrick felt seen in a way that surprised him.

"You've got something special," Dean said after a moment. "I can already see it—a natural talent."

Patrick flushed, his chest tightening slightly in surprise. "Thanks," he murmured.

They walked a bit farther in companionable quiet. Then Patrick glanced over. "What about you? Why acting?"

Dean exhaled through his nose. "Honestly? My sister. She was the born performer. Took over every room. I just learned her lines to annoy her. Somewhere along the way, I realized I liked it."

Patrick smiled. "Sibling rivalry. The gateway drug to the arts."

Dean laughed. "And my parents weren't thrilled. Doctors. Very practical people. They're still adjusting to the idea."

"I get that," Patrick said. "My dad still thinks the pinnacle of my career was kindergarten T-ball. He's not wrong, technically. I did hit the ball once."

Dean let out a surprised laugh, loud and genuine, and Patrick felt warmth bubble in his chest.

They kept walking.

They reached the Tube station. The familiar red and blue roundel glowed in the dark like a beacon. Patrick half-wished it were further away.

"Well, this is me," Dean said, nodding toward the steps. His hands were still tucked in his jacket pockets, but his shoulders hesitated, lingering.

Patrick mirrored the pause. "Thanks for tonight. Really."

"It was my pleasure," Dean said. "You're excellent cinema company."

Patrick smirked. "It's the popcorn etiquette. I share just enough to seem generous without giving you all the good bits."

"That's a delicate balance."

"I've trained for years."

Dean smiled, then sobered slightly. "If you don't mind me asking...who bailed on you tonight?"

Patrick blinked. The question wasn't aggressive. It was

soft, quiet, like Dean had been holding it all evening and only now trusted the moment enough to ask.

He considered brushing it off, making a joke. But Dean was looking at him so openly, so kindly, that the truth slipped out before he could second-guess it.

"It was someone I'd started seeing in New York. Nothing serious—at least I didn't think it was. But I was hopeful. And then literally hours after I landed here, he texted me to say he had a long-term girlfriend the whole time he was seeing me. Said he was sorry, and that was it."

Dean winced. "Oof. That's brutal."

"Yeah. Welcome to London, right? Here's your heartbreak starter pack. Comes with a side of jet lag and humiliation."

"I'm sorry, Patrick."

There was a pause. And then, without asking, Dean stepped forward and hugged him.

It wasn't awkward or performative. Just a simple, human hug. Warm and firm, his arms solid around Patrick's back, steady and grounding.

Patrick stiffened for a beat, startled. Then let himself lean into it.

Patrick suppressed a noise that might have ruined his dignity forever. Dean was solid. Dean was doing that thumb-rubbing thing on Patrick's back. He felt his dignity dissolving in real-time. If this continued, he wouldn't just melt; he'd evaporate.

Dean smelled good. That clean cedar and rain scent again. And felt like calm. Not the kind of calm you fake, but the kind that sneaks up on you. The kind you believe in, even if just for a second.

He didn't know the last time someone had hugged him like that. Not just out of comfort but instinct. It was maddening. And unfair. And really, really lovely.

Patrick could feel his ribs unclench.

When they pulled apart, Dean still had that furrow between his brows, the one that said he cared more than he let on.

"You didn't deserve that," he said.

"I know," Patrick replied. "But I'm also trying not to spiral into the self-pity montage. I've already done the sad airport playlist and the passive-aggressive journaling. I think I've hit my emotional cliché quota for the week."

Dean chuckled. "Fair. But still, he's an idiot."

Patrick raised an eyebrow. "Careful. That's dangerously close to flattery."

"I'll allow it just this once."

A train rumbled below, distant and hollow. Dean looked toward the entrance, then back at him.

"We should do this again sometime. Not necessarily *Star Wars*. But…something."

Something. The word hit like a small spark behind Patrick's ribs.

He wanted to play it cool, keep things light. But his

brain, treacherous bastard that it was, had already started writing alternate universes. Dates that weren't dates. Movie nights that turned into something more. Dean's hoodie on his floor.

"I'd like that," he said. And meant it. And panicked slightly the second he said it.

Dean nodded, then took a few steps backward toward the stairs. "Don't let the usher find you loitering. He'll start quoting Fellini."

Patrick smiled. "I'll tell him you lured me here under false pretenses."

"That tracks."

And with one last crooked smile, Dean disappeared down the steps, swallowed by the soft hum of the Underground.

Patrick stood there a moment longer, the chill creeping into his collar, but his chest oddly warm.

He turned slowly, walking back toward Notting Hill, shoes quiet against the pavement. The streetlamps cast long shadows, stretching in front of him like a path he wasn't quite sure he was meant to follow yet. But it felt good to move. To breathe.

He shoved his hands in his coat pockets, feeling the crumpled Maltesers wrapper and the faintest echo of Dean's scent on his jacket sleeve.

"God, he's annoyingly nice," Patrick muttered aloud, voice echoing softly off the shopfronts. "Of course he hugged me like that. Of course he smells like a forest after it rains. Of course he didn't make it weird."

He glanced up at the moon.

"Is the universe trying to fuck with me?"

No reply. Just a passing double-decker and a slight breeze like laughter.

Still, tonight had been good. Honest. Unexpected.

It wasn't a date. Not technically. Not officially.

But maybe it didn't need to be.

Maybe, just maybe, it was something better. The start of something he hadn't let himself hope for in a long time.

Patrick walked on, heart a little steadier, steps a little lighter.

CHAPTER 8

The first week at RADA wasn't merely a whirlwind; it was a Category 5 hurricane of theatrical intensity, a relentless, exhilarating assault on every sense. By the second week, Patrick had stopped trying to survive the storm and started learning how to breathe underwater.

Their first official monologue session began with Garrett, their main instructor and resident theatrical scalpel, prowling the front of the rehearsal room like a lion sizing up his next meal. He spoke slowly, deliberately, his voice low and commanding.

"The monologue," he said, letting the word breathe in the room, "is not just a performance. It's a confession. It's an unraveling. It's you, naked, with nothing but language to clothe your soul."

One by one, they took to the floor. Some fumbled. Some soared. It was a full-blown clusterfuck of accents, egos, and Elizabethan vowels. Jacob went first, delivering a feverish rendition of something vaguely Shakespearean with the energy of a man auditioning for an energy drink commercial. Garrett raised one eyebrow, said nothing, and moved on.

When it was Patrick's turn, something shifted. He stepped forward, spine straight, breath shallow. The text was Edmund from *King Lear*, "Thou, Nature, art my goddess." He'd chosen it for the defiance, the wound buried in intellect. But when he spoke, it felt less like recitation and more like excavation. His voice landed heavier than he expected, echoing just a bit in the silence.

When he finished, there was a pause.

Garrett nodded once. "Good. Again tomorrow. But deeper."

It was the closest thing to praise anyone had gotten all morning.

The exhaustion after class wasn't just physical; it was something else, something soul-deep. Still he floated a bit when they left the room, Jess catching up with him by the staircase.

"You cracked him," she said, nudging his shoulder. "Garrett. He made a sound. That counts as a standing ovation."

Patrick smiled faintly. "I think it was more a cough."

"Take the win, New York. Take the win."

The days blurred into a montage of exhaustion and exhilaration.

Movement classes were a dizzying ballet of

awkwardness and eventual, grudging grace. Patrick stretched muscles he hadn't known existed, discovering a sacred ache in his hips that told him he was either becoming an artist or rapidly aging.

Then came the text analysis sessions: dense, cerebral dives into Shakespearean verse where Patrick found himself clinging to words like lifeboats. The iambic pentameter beat in his head at night like a second pulse.

It was all so different from the aimless, gray days he'd left behind in New York. Back there time had felt stagnant, soupy. Here it moved in great, gulping strides. And through the chaos, the Fortune group began to solidify.

There was Jess with her razor-sharp eyeliner and even sharper tongue; Jacob, who had the enthusiasm of a Jack Russell terrier and the volume to match; Olivia, ethereal and seemingly always five seconds away from bursting into tears (or laughter, depending on the scene); and, of course, Dean.

Patrick still wasn't sure how to feel about Dean. Or rather, he knew exactly how he felt, and that was the problem.

They'd started eating lunch together in the same spot of the RADA cafeteria each day, a sticky corner near the window that smelled vaguely of industrial dish soap and overcooked broccoli. Jess had claimed it with the authority of someone who had been here in another life.

"Did you see Jacob's monologue this morning?" Jess

asked one afternoon, forking a pile of wilted spinach onto her tray like it had personally wronged her. "It was like watching *Hamlet* performed by a confused fitness instructor."

Patrick laughed into his tea. "He made 'To be or not to be' sound like an advert for a protein shake."

"A protein shake with serious abandonment issues," Jess replied, deadpan.

Across the room, a tall boy with unruly curls waved at Jess. She waved back without hesitation.

"Who's that?" Patrick asked.

"That's Monty," Jess explained, a fond look in her eyes. "He's in the Perdita group. We did a scene together last week. He's great—you'll love him. He's really funny."

Patrick filed that away. Another character to study.

Jess turned back to him, her expression shifting. "But yours? Garrett looked like he might...actually smile."

Patrick flushed. "You're exaggerating."

"Please. I saw the corner of his mouth twitch. That's practically a confetti cannon in Garrett-speak."

He stirred his tea. It had gone cold again. He didn't mind. The nerves were louder than his taste buds.

"I just...channeled some things, I guess. Recent life decisions. Being dumped by someone and then moving across the ocean to chase ghosts and Shakespeare."

Jess nodded, eyes softening. "That'll do it."

He hesitated, then plunged ahead. "Speaking of...*complicated* people. What do you think of Dean?"

Her eyebrows shot up. "Dean?"

"Our resident mystery novel. That hair. The brooding. The fact that he reads Brecht like it's erotica."

Jess gave a slow, theatrical sip of her coffee. "He's got that James Dean thing going on. It's not just the cheekbones, either. It's the whole quiet intensity thing. He looks like he's constantly about to have a life-altering epiphany."

Patrick sighed. "He's actually...lovely. Like, genuinely kind. And smart. And annoyingly talented."

Jess tilted her head. "You like him."

He tried to deflect, but it was pointless.

"It's just...I keep catching myself watching him in class. Not in a creepy way. In a curious way. Like, how does he get that stillness? That control? And then sometimes he'll glance over and smile like he knows I'm spiraling."

"Have you talked to him about anything other than iambic pentameter?"

Patrick hesitated for just a moment too long.

"We actually went to the movies the other night," he said finally.

Jess's fork froze midair. "Wait, what? Like, the two of you? Alone?"

He nodded, trying to sound nonchalant. "Yeah. That place on Portobello Road. They were playing *Empire Strikes*

Back. My original plan... Well, the guy bailed. So I asked Dean last minute after our first class, and he said yes."

Her eyes widened. "Patrick! That's a date. That's a literal date. You invited him after being stood up, and he showed up—looking good, I assume?"

Patrick gave her a look. "It's Dean. Of course, he looked good. It was a lot."

Jess dropped her fork with a clatter. "Jesus Christ, you are hopeless. You're living in a Richard Curtis film, and you don't even know it."

Patrick laughed, but his heart was thudding again. It had felt a little like a date. Or maybe he just wanted it to.

"Do you think he likes me?" he asked, quieter this time.

"I think," Jess said, leaning in, "he's halfway to writing you a sonnet. And if he's not, I will on his behalf."

Before Patrick could respond, Jess's eyes flicked to something, or someone, just over his shoulder.

"And speak of the beautiful devil," she muttered.

They both straightened in unison, posture suddenly pristine, expressions neutral but not too neutral, each of them clearly trying to look as if they hadn't just been deeply dissecting the romantic viability of the man now walking toward them.

Dean, of course, looked annoyingly good in a navy sweater, probably the same one, curls slightly mussed, that easy warmth already radiating from him.

"Hey," he said, sliding into the seat beside Patrick like

he belonged there.

Patrick hoped to God he wasn't still blushing.

Dean set his tray down beside Patrick's, giving Jess a quick nod before turning to him with that maddeningly unreadable smile.

"You survived Garrett," Dean said. "Congratulations. Your eyebrows didn't even twitch once."

Patrick forced a chuckle. "It was touch and go. I think I blacked out around the fourth iamb."

"Patrick made him nod," Jess interjected, like she was reporting breaking news. "Not just nod. Nod and say something vaguely human."

Dean raised an impressed eyebrow. "High praise from the man himself. Did he say it in full sentences or just grunt and float out of the room like a disgruntled phantom?"

"Somewhere in between," Patrick replied. "He said, 'Good. Again tomorrow. But deeper.' Which I think is his version of foreplay."

Jess snorted iced coffee out her nose. Dean grinned, and Patrick's stomach did something treacherous and fluttery.

They fell into easy rhythm, the three of them trading stories from movement class and speculating on whether Olivia had secretly trained with Cirque du Soleil.

"She did a backbend that made my spine consider early retirement," Dean said, picking at his sandwich. "I think she levitated."

Jess leaned across the table. "Okay, but more importantly, Dean, would you or would you not survive a zombie apocalypse?"

Dean blinked, mid-bite. "What kind of question is that?"

"A vital one," she replied. "We're forming a survival plan. Jacob's out. He talks too much. Olivia might float away. Patrick's in if he learns how to run without flailing."

Patrick raised his hands. "I flail with intention."

Dean considered. "I think I'd survive. But like...brooding in a church tower. Rationing canned beans. Journaling about morality."

Jess grinned. "Yeah, I could see that."

Her phone buzzed on the tray beside her. She glanced down, frowned, and sighed the way only someone who had just seen "urgent rehearsal reschedule" in a group chat could.

"Well, my apocalypse will have to wait. I've been summoned to Room 3B for what I can only assume is an interpretive dance about grief."

She stood, gathering her tray, then paused to give Patrick a loaded look.

"You boys behave."

Dean gave her a mock salute. "No promises."

As she walked off, she shot Patrick a subtle thumbs-up behind Dean's back. He nearly snorted.

And then it was just the two of them.

Cue internal panic.

Patrick sipped his tea to stall. Still cold. Still awful. He sipped it again.

Dean sat back in his chair, eyes sweeping the room for a beat before landing back on Patrick.

"You okay? You've gone kind of...quiet in the eyes."

"I'm fine," Patrick said quickly. "Just recalibrating to solo conversational mode."

Dean smiled, easy and lopsided. "I get it. Jess is like being hit by a very charming truck."

They fell into silence for a moment, not awkward, but not entirely comfortable either. Patrick tried not to read into it. He was definitely not imagining a soundtrack swelling underneath this cafeteria chatter. Definitely not waiting for Dean to say something cinematic.

"So," Dean said finally. "Did you like the movie?"

Ah. There it was.

"I did," Patrick replied, a little too quickly. "Even if I was bracing for you to judge my emotional response to Chewbacca."

"I would never judge Chewbacca-based emotions," Dean said, mock-offended. "He is adorable and weirdly intense. Like me on a bad day."

Patrick chuckled. "You didn't even blink when Darth Vader said he was Luke's father. Have you just seen it that many times, or are you dead inside?"

"Bit of both," Dean said, "but mostly, I was trying not

to look like I was watching you watching the movie."

Patrick blinked. "Sorry…what?"

Dean's cheeks colored slightly, but he didn't look away. "You make really expressive faces when you're into something. Or when you're pretending not to be."

Patrick felt every molecule in his body go incandescent. He scrambled for a witty comeback, something dry and self-deprecating.

What came out was, "Cool. Good. Love that for me."

Dean laughed. "You're so weird."

There was another beat of silence. This one felt different. Tenuous. Like something balancing on a wire.

Before either of them could say something they couldn't unsay, Jacob plopped into Jess's recently vacated seat with the subtlety of a marching band, unwrapping a sandwich like it had personally insulted him.

Of course. Florida Man arrives right on cue, Patrick thought, watching the serene tension between him and Dean dissolve like sugar in tea.

"Did I miss anything? Did anyone cry?" Jacob said loudly.

Dean leaned back slightly, but his knee brushed Patrick's under the table again. Neither of them moved it.

"Nope," Patrick said, keeping his face neutral. "You missed exactly nothing."

Jacob nodded, clearly satisfied, and dove into his sandwich with zero awareness of the mood he'd just steamrolled.

Patrick didn't even bother looking at Dean. He could feel the smirk sitting just behind his eyes.

Moment: ruined. But maybe just for now.

Dean cleared his throat lightly. "Well, Patrick and I should probably get going."

Patrick blinked. "Going?"

Dean nodded, standing. "Yeah. That thing."

Patrick was on his feet before his brain caught up. "Right. The thing. Very urgent."

They made their exit without fanfare, trays abandoned, Jacob still mid-sandwich and oblivious.

As they stepped into the hallway, Patrick leaned over and muttered, "Smooth. That was almost presidential."

Dean grinned. "You looked like you were seconds away from setting yourself on fire."

"I was. It felt metaphorically appropriate."

They walked in comfortable silence past rehearsal rooms and open doors spilling out snippets of verse and piano scales.

"Actually," Dean said, stopping and checking his watch. "Since we have 'that thing' to do...which currently consists of absolutely nothing...would you want to run lines now? Before the *Romeo and Juliet* auditions?"

"I'd love that," Patrick said.

"Great," Dean said, eyes twinkling. "But first, I'm

taking you on a tour. A real one. None of that tourist nonsense. We're starting with St. James's Park."

"Wait, now?"

"Now," Dean said, already walking. "Keep up, New York."

The "tour" turned into two hours, three questionable pigeons, and several helpings of gelato Patrick immediately regretted.

"This isn't rehearsal," Patrick said as they crossed a footbridge near St. James's Park. "This is cardio disguised as cultural enrichment."

"You'll thank me when you're cast as a prince who broods near a fountain," Dean said, smirking.

"God forbid I ever play a straight man in period tights."

"You'd slay in tights."

"Slay?" Patrick said, wide-eyed.

"Isn't that what all the cool kids are saying nowadays?" Dean said, grinning.

Patrick laughed. He couldn't help it.

Dean pointed out monuments like he'd built them himself, narrating each one with a mix of Wikipedia trivia and emotionally repressed charm. It was annoying how charming it was.

They watched ducks paddle through murky water while Patrick resisted the urge to narrate like a BBC presenter. Dean offered enthusiastic commentary on all things bird-related, which was both endearing and vaguely alarming.

"You're really into the fauna here," Patrick said.

"There's something very grounding about a bird that looks like it could survive a nuclear winter," Dean said, shrugging.

"Yeah, or start one," Patrick said, glancing at the massive beaked dinosaur lurching toward a sandwich wrapper.

Dean smiled, not just with his mouth, but his eyes crinkled slightly at the corners. Patrick tried not to stare.

Later came Trafalgar Square, where the pigeons had even less regard for human dignity.

"They're attracted to your resting empathy face," Dean said, dodging one midair.

"I'm serious," he added. "They sense you're soft."

"New York pigeons would eat these guys for breakfast. With a side of bagel," Patrick said, swatting the air.

Dean snorted, and Patrick grinned. It was effortless with him. And maybe that was the problem.

They ended up in front of a bright red phone booth. Dean insisted on a photo. He tossed an arm around Patrick's shoulders like it was nothing, like this was what people did, and Patrick forgot how to stand still for five full seconds.

Later, looking at the photo on his phone, he noticed the way he leaned into Dean's side. He told himself it didn't mean anything. That he was just off balance. That Dean probably hadn't noticed.

Which made it even more annoying when he did.

Their rehearsals in Patrick's small, surprisingly cozy room at Schaffer House evolved from academic necessity into a sanctuary, a carved-out space inside the grind of RADA.

Lines for *Romeo and Juliet* sprawled across the twin bed, among a landscape of discarded tea mugs, half-eaten biscuits, and dog-eared scripts that seemed to multiply overnight, each one a stamp of shared dedication.

They often wrestled playfully over pages, their hands reaching for the same line, Dean's fingers brushing Patrick's and sending a quick electric current up his arm that he pretended not to notice.

"This dagger prop is janky," Patrick said, scowling as he tried to unsheathe a stiff plastic knife. "It is actively resisting my will to look menacing. How am I supposed to deliver a convincing '*Et tu, Brute?*' with a glorified butter knife?"

"It is not janky; it is aged with character," Dean said, chuckling as he took the prop. "That is the key to British props. You must act through adversity. Let it teach you the quiet desperation of a dying man. Again. And try to look less like you have discovered a particularly pungent cheddar."

"Right," he said, taking his script. "Balcony scene

again."

Dean's teasing faded into a calm intensity. He leaned by the window, evening light along his profile, and began.

Dean (Romeo):

> "But, soft! what light through yonder window breaks?
>
> It is the east, and Julius is the sun."

Patrick felt his pulse quicken. The familiar lines carried new weight, a yearning that was not entirely the scene's. He looked at Dean, at the open sincerity in his face, and let the words sit in his own mouth as if they had always been there.

Patrick (Juliet):

> "O Romeo, Romeo, wherefore art thou Romeo?
>
> Deny thy father and refuse thy name;
>
> Or, if thou wilt not, be but sworn my love,
>
> And I'll no longer be a Capulet."

He broke character with a crooked smile.

"Seriously, why do you have to be Romeo?" Patrick said.

Dean stayed in character for a beat, perfect mock suffering drifting into actual amusement. He leaned in and whispered, "It is the deep, profound, existential suffering of having a name that is not quite right. A truly relatable plight."

"Okay, fair. But also, 'Tis but thy name that is my

enemy.' I feel that. It's like my dating life in New York. The names are the problem, never the person. Right?" Patrick said.

Dean (Romeo):

>"What's in a name? That which we call a rose
>By any other word would smell as sweet;
>So Romeo would, were he not Romeo call'd,
>Retain that dear perfection which he owes
>Without that title."

Patrick's breath hitched. That was not Shakespeare. He felt a blush rise and forced himself back to the page.

Dean (Romeo):

>"I take thee at thy word:
>Call me but love, and I'll be new baptized;
>Henceforth I never will be Romeo."

Patrick (Juliet):

>"What man art thou that, thus bescreen'd in night,
>So stumblest on my counsel?"

Dean (Romeo):

>"By a name
>I know not how to tell thee who I am:
>My name, dear saint, is hateful to myself, Because
>it is an enemy to thee."

They held the moment too long for classroom comfort, unsaid words hanging between them, the room briefly charged. Dean's eyes, full of a quiet, steady yearning, searched Patrick's face, and a question rose without language.

Then Dean stepped back, cleared his throat, and let the current ease.

"Right. Good. Your line lands. That is solid," he said, giving a small, nervous smile.

Patrick nodded, his voice somewhere far down the elevator shaft of his chest. The moment had been both a clean scene and a wordless admission.

Between scenes, they sprawled on the floor, sharing earbuds. Dean insisted Patrick learn the foundations: Oasis, Bowie, The Who. Patrick volleyed back with American folk, punk, and pop, and Dean surprised him by knowing half of it already, complete with take-no-prisoners opinions on a current chart-topper.

They were supposed to call it after rehearsals. Dean had a paper due, and Patrick had promised himself he'd do laundry before his socks staged a coup. But as Dean stretched and slung an arm behind his head, eyes catching Patrick's with an amused gleam, he said, "You hungry?"

"Starving," Patrick said.

"Let's get a bite. Somewhere close. You deserve a proper meal after that balcony scene," Dean said.

And that's how they ended up at Gig's, a cozy, unassuming fish and chips spot tucked just down Tottenham Street from RADA.

The name sounded like a clandestine meeting place,

which suited them.

Inside, the smell of malt vinegar and fried fish mixed with ale and the soft ghosts of old conversations. Their snug corner table always seemed open, as if saved by some benevolent pub spirit. The windows stood wide on warm nights, the air moving gently with the distant murmur of the city and the occasional burst of laughter from the street.

Patrick felt true bliss sitting across from Dean, watching his animated expressions and easy charm. Between clinks of glasses and the steady hum of chatter, they shared plates of golden fish and chips, conversations flowing as easily as the beer.

Dean's rolling laughter and Patrick's unguarded smiles punctuated talk of school, the bewildering quirks of their classmates, and the absurd intricacies of British life. More than once Dean mentioned Olivia, her sharp notes in text class, the way she helped him find a cleaner turn on a tricky line, casual observations that made Patrick's stomach twist and then settle, equal parts admiration and caution.

"So, what is your drink of choice? You've handled a few pints. Time for something properly British. Beyond beer. Something that holds the spirit of a British summer," Dean said, leaning across the table, eyes gleaming.

"I like something fruity, I guess. In the States it's all craft cocktails and obscure bitters and dramatic bartenders with tragic backstories. I'm open. Surprise me. Something

British, fruity, and not a life choice I regret," Patrick said, swirling what was left of his ale.

"Pimm's Cup. The taste of a garden party without the small talk. More potential for delightful tipsiness," Dean said, brightening. He caught the bartender's eye with a confident nod.

Two tall, frosted glasses arrived, brimming with ice, cucumber, orange, mint, and a ruby liquid that looked like bottled sunshine.

"Oh," Patrick said, honestly surprised. "This is really good. The kind of good that tricks you into thinking it's fancy lemonade, and suddenly you're singing show tunes and recruiting strangers for a flash mob."

"Told you," Dean said, satisfied. "The taste of British summer. Also the taste of British regret if you have too many. A rite of passage. Consider yourself officially inducted."

There were many. The Pimm's flowed, and so did the conversation, looping from silly to personal, from Shakespeare to childhood stories and future wishes.

By the time they stepped into the cool London night, the streets had quieted. Lamplight cast long shadows that stretched and swayed as they walked. Patrick felt the alcohol loosen the knot in his chest until Dean dropped the bomb.

"You know who's actually brilliant?" Dean said suddenly. "Olivia. We were working on a scene today and she just... She has this presence. You can't look away from her. She's got that old-school beauty. Just effortless."

Patrick paused, his glass halfway to his mouth. He felt a sharp, cold prick in his chest.

"She really is," Dean went on, shaking his head with a little too much admiration. "Magnetic. It's kind of intimidating, actually."

Patrick forced a nod.

"So talented," Patrick agreed out loud, his voice tight.

He needed to know. He needed to touch the bruise.

"So, dating life. Mine has been a disaster. Just one in a long string of catastrophes," Patrick said, trying to sound casual. "What about you?" Patrick asked, lifted by liquid courage and sudden curiosity. "Any dramatic exes? Or just faded away, like a bad summer tan with questionable lines and lingering regret?"

"Mostly faded," Dean said, sighing and leaning beside him, the lamplight skimming the faint stubble along his jaw. "I had one serious girlfriend—Chloe. We dated for a few years back when I was deciding between acting, professional tea tasting, or becoming a very well-read hermit in a Scottish cottage, communing with the sheep.

"She was lovely. My best friend. It ran its course. No drama, no shouting—just a quiet fizzle. More friendship than fire by the end. A mutual understanding," he said, chuckling.

"But you're good, Dean. You belong here," Patrick

said, feeling a pang and unfairly, a flash of hope. The ease with which Dean described a gentle ending spoke of warmth, not heat. It made Patrick's chest float.

"So, just girlfriends?" Patrick asked, casual in tone but not at all casual inside. His heart thumped hard, a drum solo that would not sit back down.

"But Patrick," Dean said softly, almost a whisper, "listening to your stories, you have this capacity for life, for feeling things deeply. You're going to find the man of your dreams. You deserve it. You're incredible. And you deserve someone who truly sees that and loves you for it, without reservation."

It was a beautiful thing to say.

It was also, Patrick realized with a sinking feeling, exactly what you say to someone you are putting in the "friend" zone. It was a compliment that doubled as a wall.

"Thanks," Patrick said, forcing a smile. "That means a lot."

"Come on. I'll walk you back to Schaffer," Dean said, shifting, not unkindly.

They drifted down the pavement, tipsy and careful, a few inches apart, the unspoken still present between them, close and far at the same time.

"You know, when my sister was in school, she was always in plays. The lead. The spotlight. I'd just sit backstage with a book. Everyone thought I liked it that way," Dean said as they neared Schaffer House.

"That you'd be the quiet one?" Patrick asked softly.

"The one who'd do something solid. Predictable. Something with results. Both my parents, they're doctors, remember? So when I said I wanted to act, it was like I'd suggested clown school. They smiled. They nodded. But I could feel them recalibrating their whole image of me," Dean said with a small huff of laughter. "I guess I'm saying... I didn't grow up thinking someone like me got to want this. Let alone do it."

"You're good, Dean. You belong here," Patrick said, his chest tightening.

"So do you," Dean said, meeting his eyes.

BUZZ. BUZZ.

Dean stiffened. He pulled back, not abruptly but with a heavy, resigned sigh.

He reached into his pocket and pulled out his phone. The screen lit up his face in a harsh blue glow.

Patrick watched Dean's shoulders slump. For a split second, the charm vanished.

"Everything okay?" Patrick asked softly.

Dean blinked, and just like that, the curtain went back up.

He shoved the phone back into his pocket and forced a smile. It was a good smile—practiced, polite, charming— but it didn't reach his eyes. The vulnerability from a moment ago had been plastered over with a layer of perfect, porcelain "fine."

"Oh, yeah," Dean said, his voice bright. "Just family stuff."

He took a small step back, creating a polite distance.

"I should actually probably take this," Dean said, apologetic. "Sorry to cut the night short. But... thank you. For the Pimm's. For the walk."

"Dean, you sure you're—"

"I'm great," Dean interrupted, the smile widening, becoming brittle. "Really. Go get some sleep. You've got a monologue to crush tomorrow."

He gave a quick, reassuring wave and turned away.

He answered the phone as he walked down the street, his voice dropping low, his posture rigid.

Patrick stood alone on the sidewalk.

"And scene," he muttered as he turned and walked into the dorms.

CHAPTER 9

The day of the *Romeo and Juliet* cast announcement landed at RADA like a low-pressure system: thick, breathless, and vaguely apocalyptic. Students buzzed through the hallways with the jittery energy of people who'd forgotten how to blink. Patrick had tried to act cool, even brought snacks, as if that proved he was above the drama, but the half-eaten sandwich in his lap betrayed the lie.

He was sitting cross-legged near the call board, picking at the edges of the crust, trying not to replay the end of last night on a loop. Dean had practically run away after that phone call, looking terrified.

Patrick had expected things to be weird today. He had expected silence or awkward avoidance.

Instead, when he'd walked into movement class that morning, Dean was leaning against the back wall, sipping a coffee and looking suspiciously unbothered.

"Dean?" Patrick had asked, stepping closer, voice

lowered. "Hey. About last night… Are you okay? You took off pretty fast."

Dean straightened up, flashing a smile so blindingly normal it felt like a weapon.

"Me? I'm fantastic," Dean said, clapping Patrick on the shoulder. "Everything is fine. Honestly, don't worry about it. I had a great time yesterday. The tour? The Pimm's? Top tier."

"Right," Patrick said, searching Dean's eyes for a crack in the facade. "But the phone call—"

"Family drama. Bore you to tears," Dean interrupted, his smile not wavering for a second. "Anyway, big day. Cast list. Fingers crossed, yeah?"

And then he'd tossed his empty cup in the bin and jogged over to join the warm-up circle without looking back.

It was a masterclass in deflection. Dean had just slammed the door in his face, but he'd done it with such a winning smile that Patrick almost thanked him for it.

Someone flopped down beside him near the call board with the force of a stage combat roll, jarring him from his thoughts.

"Right," said the boy, dramatically winded, "if I'm Nurse, you owe me your firstborn and half your closet."

Patrick looked over. It took a second to register Monty, all kinetic energy and curly hair and chaos incarnate. They hadn't spoken much beyond class comments and shared

Jess proximity, but Patrick knew him by reputation. Loud, funny, endlessly charming in a way that seemed like it should be exhausting but wasn't.

"Monty, right?" Patrick asked, wiping sandwich crumbs off his hands.

"Only when I'm not being 'deeply unhinged energy personified,' as Jess so kindly phrased it."

"She says it with affection," Patrick said with a snort.

"She better. I'm her unofficial emotional support clown."

It was meant as a joke, but Patrick caught the way Monty glanced toward the hallway, like maybe he was hoping Jess would appear. He tucked that away, one more detail to puzzle out later.

Monty leaned back against the wall, legs sprawled like he owned the building. "Anyway. Tell me: if you're cast as Juliet, are you emotionally prepared to die in my arms eight times a week?"

"I've seen your stage crying. I'd die of secondhand embarrassment before the poison even kicks in," Patrick said.

Monty gasped, clutching his chest. "Rude. My emotional range has been described as devastating by at least two exes and a dog I briefly fostered."

"Devastating like a tornado or devastating like a sad indie film?"

"Trick question," Monty said, chewing the end of a

gummy bear he'd pulled from his pocket. "I'm both. I contain multitudes."

Patrick laughed, real, surprised laughter. For someone he barely knew, Monty had a way of cutting through anxiety like a well-timed monologue.

"Okay, but real talk," Monty said, dropping the bit for a moment. "What's your guess? Casting-wise?"

"Dean's getting Romeo," Patrick said after a pause.

"Obviously. He broods like it's a vocational skill. And the lighting in that last monologue workshop? Tragic perfection."

"No arguments here," Patrick said, biting back a smile.

Monty gave him a once-over. "You, though—you've got chemistry. Not just the lines. Like, capital-R Romantic energy. I've seen you rehearse. You feel stuff. People notice."

"Thanks," Patrick said, flushing. He wanted to believe it. He really did.

"I, on the other hand, will be thrilled if I get Nurse. All I want is comedic relief and an emotionally confusing wig."

"I'd pay to see that."

"You will. I charge friends full price."

Patrick laughed again. Somehow, this absurd little moment was calming him more than any deep breathing exercise. Monty wasn't just funny; he was warm, observant, and a little sharper than he let on.

A beat passed. Then Monty added, almost offhand,

"I'm not great at wanting things. But I think I might actually want this."

Patrick looked over. The humor was still there, but it was tempered now, softer around the edges. He nudged Monty's shoulder with his.

"You're going to be amazing. Whatever part you get."

"Said like someone who's about to crush the balcony scene and make us all cry," Monty said with a grin.

"Let's not get ahead of ourselves."

They stood up as the hallway buzzed louder, the cast list imminent. Monty glanced around one last time, maybe still hoping for Jess. Patrick noticed.

He filed it away.

At precisely 2:58 PM, the common room was packed. A buzzing, anxious throng of students milled around, faces tight with anticipation, a hundred nervous glances cast toward the door. Patrick stood with Jess near the windows, trying to ground himself with deep breaths. His hand kept clenching and unclenching at his side, a nervous tic that had taken up permanent residence over the past forty-eight hours.

Dean was a few feet away, talking quietly with Olivia. Their heads were angled in toward each other in a way that made something twist at the base of Patrick's ribs. Olivia's expression was calm and unreadable, but the kind that clocked everything. She rested a hand lightly on Dean's arm and said something too quiet to hear. Dean nodded, focused, something serious flashing in his face before smoothing into a polite smile.

Patrick looked away.

At 3:00 on the dot, Garrett entered the room, holding a single sheet of paper as if it were the nuclear launch codes.

"Alright," he said, voice even, commanding. "First off, well done. I know I say that every time, but truly, this round of auditions was exceptional. But casting is a puzzle. We aren't just looking for talent; we are looking for friction. For chemistry that challenges."

The room tensed.

Garrett let the moment hang in the air a second longer before consulting the page in his hand.

"We'll start with the supporting players," Garrett said.

"For Mercutio…Jessica Montez."

Jess let out a sharp intake of breath and squeezed Patrick's arm hard enough to leave a bruise.

"For the Nurse…Montgomery Price."

A delighted whoop erupted from the back of the room. Monty executed an exaggerated curtsy that made half the room laugh.

"For Benvolio…Olivia Hart."

Garrett continued down the list, rattling off names for Tybalt, the Friar, the Capulets. The list was shrinking. The air in the room felt thin.

"And for the role of Paris," Garrett read, his eyes briefly flicking to Patrick.

"Patrick O'Connell."

Paris.

The safe choice. The boring choice. The guy in the nice suit who gets left at the altar because he isn't interesting enough to die for.

It felt like a physical slap.

Fuck, Patrick thought.

He nodded, forcing a smile that felt pasted on.

Garrett cleared his throat. The room went dead silent.

"Now, for the leads," Garrett said. "As you know, I like to experiment. I like to push boundaries. For this production, we will be exploring a different dynamic. We will be performing *Romeo and Julius.* Two male leads."

Patrick's heart jumped. Two male leads. He looked at Dean.

"For the role of Julius…" Garrett paused.

"…Jacob Vance."

The air left Patrick's lungs.

There was a beat of silence, followed by a confused ripple of applause.

"Yes!" Jacob yelled, pumping a fist in the air. "Julius! Let's go!"

Patrick was frozen.

Double fuck.

Jacob. The energy drink enthusiast. The man who treated Shakespeare like a contact sport.

"And for the role of Romeo," Garrett finished, looking calm amidst the chaos. "Dean Clarke."

A wave of applause broke out, louder this time. It was the correct choice. Everyone knew it.

"Congratulations to all," Garrett said, raising his voice slightly over the noise. "We will post the full rehearsal schedule later today. Be ready to work tomorrow."

He turned and marched out, leaving the room to dissolve into chaos.

Patrick stood still while the room celebrated around him. He felt hollowed out. Crushed. It wasn't just disappointment; it was humiliation. He had convinced himself that the chemistry with Dean meant something.

"Congrats, mate!" Jacob boomed, grabbing Dean in a headlock. "We've got some work to do. I'm thinking Julius is gritty, you know?"

Patrick briefly considered finding the nearest alligator in a Florida swamp and slapping Jacob across the fucking face with it.

Dean looked like he was being mauled by a dog. He extricated himself from Jacob's grip, his eyes searching the room until they found Patrick.

Dean didn't look happy. He looked apologetic.

"Paris," Jess hissed in his ear, sounding furious on his behalf. "Are you kidding me? Paris? It's a piece of cardboard in a doublet."

"It's a good role," Patrick lied.

"Patrick."

Dean was there. He looked genuinely gutted.

"Hey," Dean said softly.

"Congrats on Romeo," Patrick said. He was proud of how steady his voice was.

"It's ridiculous," Dean muttered, low enough that Jacob couldn't hear. "You should be Julius. Everyone knows it."

"Well, Garrett doesn't think so. And he's the director." Patrick shrugged.

Dean opened his mouth to argue, but Jacob barreled into them.

"Dean! We need to start running lines! I've got ideas for the balcony scene. Physicality, right?"

Patrick watched Dean's soul leave his body.

"Right," Dean said weakly. "Physicality."

"I'm gonna grab a celebratory drink," Patrick said, backing away. "You guys...bond."

"Wait," Dean said, panic flaring in his eyes. "We're all going. The Italian place across the street. Dinner. You have to come."

"I don't think—"

"Please," Dean said. And there it was again. That vulnerability. "I want you there."

Patrick sighed.

"Fine. But I'm ordering the most expensive thing on the menu."

The plan to "grab a quick bite" turned into a full-blown celebratory dinner at a small, family-run Italian place a few blocks from the school.

Patrick, Jess, Monty, and Dean crammed into a corner booth near the window. Jacob pulled up a chair at the head of the table, acting very much the leading man.

Jess was in full sparkle mode, dramatic reenactments of everyone's auditions spilling from her like wine. "I swear to God, Monty, your take on the Nurse was, like, spiritually offensive to Shakespeare. And I mean that as the highest possible compliment."

"Thank you. I draw inspiration from my nana's church friends. Big, bold, and emotionally fragile," Monty said.

Patrick laughed, but he felt like he was watching the scene through a glass wall.

Across the table, Dean kept catching his eye, offering small, sympathetic smiles that hurt more than if he'd just ignored him.

Somewhere between the ravioli and the tiramisu, Jess stood. "Okay, Monty and I are heading to the pub for one drink and mild gossiping. You two want to come?"

"I'm good here, I think," Dean said, glancing at Patrick.

"Yeah, I kind of like this table," Patrick said.

Jacob stood up, wiping tomato sauce from his mouth. "I'm coming with you guys. Gotta celebrate the lead role properly. Dean, Julius commands you to rest."

"Julius commands," Dean muttered into his wine.

"Suit yourselves," Jess said.

They left in a burst of laughter and perfume. And suddenly, it was just the two of them.

The noise of the restaurant faded slightly.

"I'm sorry," Dean said immediately. "About the casting. It's wrong."

"It is what it is," Patrick said, swirling the last of his wine. "Maybe I'm just destined to play the guy who almost gets the guy."

"You're too good for Paris," Dean said fiercely. "You have more depth in your little finger than Jacob has in his entire 'gritty' concept."

Patrick looked up. "Thanks, Dean."

"I mean it. We're going to find moments. Paris and Romeo have scenes. We'll make them the best scenes in the play."

Patrick blinked. Before he could find a reply, the restaurant door swung open behind them.

The bell chimed softly.

Patrick turned and felt the bottom drop out of his stomach.

The universe had to be shitting him.

It was Victor.

Of course, it was Victor.

He walked in like he was stepping out of a GQ spread. Smiling like nothing ever happened. Like he hadn't vanished without a word and taken something vital with him. And he wasn't alone. A girl was with him—blonde, pretty, laughing at something he said.

"Patrick?" Dean's voice was low, concerned, a gentle question that cut through the sudden roaring in his ears. "What is it? Are you alright?"

Patrick could only manage a choked whisper. "It's...it's Victor. The guy. From New York. The one who...who ghosted me."

Dean's eyes cooled, steadying into something protective. He glanced at Victor, then back at Patrick. He clocked the panic in Patrick's eyes. He clocked the feeling of defeat that had been hanging over Patrick all afternoon.

Without a word, he reached across the table, his hand finding Patrick's, giving it a firm, reassuring squeeze.

"Right. Look at me, Patrick. Not him. And if he comes over here…" His mouth tilted into a dangerous smirk. "We will make it so awkward he'll wish he had never been born. Or at least never ghosted you. We will give him a performance he will never forget."

"Come on then. Let's really sell it. Hold my hand. Laugh. Look like you're utterly besotted with me. We'll walk by their table, and you can give him your best *I am so over you and look what I found* smile," Dean said with a grin.

"Really?" Patrick asked, shock and gratitude washing through him.

"Bloody hell, yes," Dean said, his smirk widening, mischief in his eyes. "Consider it part of my ongoing commitment to dramatic justice. And...I'm your leading man, aren't I? Even if Garrett cast the wrong Julius."

He squeezed Patrick's hand again, a silent promise of unwavering support. Patrick took a breath, felt a spark of his old self flicker back to life. With Dean beside him, radiating quiet strength and a talent for the theatrical, the situation felt less terrifying and more like a scene they could conquer together.

He managed a smile back. He squeezed Dean's hand. They stood.

Dean's hand stayed in his, fingers intertwining naturally, a comfortable, firm grip. The awareness of it was immediate and electric. This was more than pretense.

They began to walk, slowly, deliberately, a casual stroll past Victor's table. Patrick fixed a bright, effortless smile onto his face and looked up at Dean, eyes sparkling with genuine amusement and newfound daring. Dean met his gaze, his own smile soft and knowing, and let out a low chuckle, the sound of shared mischief.

As they passed Victor's table, Patrick kept his smile steady, his gaze locked with Dean's. Their hands stayed clasped as Victor's head snapped up. Surprise flashed, then confusion, then the slow dawning of recognition. His laughter died. His smile faltered. His girlfriend leaned in and whispered something, her brow pinched with a question.

They kept walking, out of the restaurant and into the cool London night, their hands still joined.

A block away, they realized they were still holding on. Patrick glanced down, then up. Dean was already looking at him. A wave of giggles bubbled up between them, part relief, part delightful awkwardness.

They let go together, their hands hovering for a beat before falling to their sides. The silence that followed wasn't awkward. It was warm, threaded with a new unspoken question and the knowledge of a line crossed.

"Should we…actually run those lines?" Dean asked, voice low. "Since we're already together."

"I suspect you just want to avoid Jacob's text messages about pull-ups," Patrick said.

"That is distinctly possible," Dean admitted.

"Yeah. I've got tea. And snacks. My place?" Patrick said.

"Lead the way, Paris," Dean said with a grin.

"Methinks thou shouldst go fuck thyself, my liege," Patrick retorted, bumping his shoulder against Dean's.

They walked off into the night, side by side, a little closer than before.

CHAPTER 10

The morning after the cast announcement was supposed to be productive. Dean had come over to Patrick's dorm after the restaurant to "run lines"—a euphemism that quickly dissolved into shared Victoria sponge cake, half-memorized monologues, and an unhinged marathon of terrible British reality TV. By the time they passed out, Dean on the floor, Patrick diagonally across the bed, it was well past 3 AM.

So when Patrick jolted awake the next morning, blinking blearily at the harsh light filtering through his curtains, something felt...wrong.

He turned to check his phone. And froze.

9:37 AM. Rehearsals had started at 9.

"Oh, fuck," he whispered, already kicking off his blankets as he rolled out of bed.

A tangle of limbs stirred on the floor. "Mmm. Five more minutes. Dream's just getting good," Dean mumbled into his pillow.

"Dean, we're late. Like, so-fucking-late-Garrett's-gonna-eat-our-hearts late."

Dean opened one eye. Registered the panic. Opened the other. "Oh, bloody hell."

They launched into a frenzied routine of dressing and tripping over themselves. Patrick nearly brained himself on the bedframe trying to pull on socks. Dean ran into the wardrobe door and cursed impressively. Patrick grabbed a half-eaten cookie off his desk and shoved it into his mouth. Dean was still buttoning his shirt as they bolted out the door.

They burst into the rehearsal hall almost an hour late, wild-eyed and breathless. The rest of the cast was already in position. Olivia was stretching with perfect poise. Jess gave them a deeply unimpressed look from the floor. Monty waved cheerfully from where he was practicing a "Nurse" faint. Garrett stood center stage with his arms crossed, looking like a disappointed god.

"Clarke. O'Connell," he said, his voice low and ominous. "Care to enlighten us on your tardiness?"

Dean offered a sheepish smile. "Deep character work. We were exploring Romeo and Julius's nocturnal habits. Very authentic."

"Yes. Very method," Patrick said, crumbs still on his chin.

Garrett's eyes narrowed to slits. "I see." He paused. "Well, Mr. Clarke, I expect your performance today to reflect that level of immersion."

He let the silence hang just long enough before adding, "Get into position. And consider this a formal warning. Punctuality is not a suggestion."

Garrett didn't let them move, however. He clapped his hands once, sharp and loud, silencing the whispers in the room.

"Before we begin the movement block, I have an announcement regarding the creative team," Garrett said, his voice projecting to the back wall. He turned his gaze directly to Patrick.

"O'Connell. Step forward."

Patrick stepped forward, heart pounding, wondering if he was about to be fired for being late.

"I have reviewed the resumes of everyone in this cast," Garrett said, addressing the room but keeping his eyes on Patrick. "And it is clear that I am wasting a significant resource by having Mr. O'Connell merely stand in the background of the dance numbers."

Garrett paused for effect.

"Therefore, I am naming Patrick as Dance Captain and Co-Choreographer for this production, effective immediately. He will run the movement warm-ups and clean the choreography. When he speaks regarding movement, you will listen as if it were me speaking."

A ripple of murmurs went through the room, mostly relief, especially from the ensemble dancers who had been struggling with the complex rhythms.

Garrett gestured to the floor. "The floor is yours, Patrick. Fix the masquerade ball. It currently looks like a pub brawl."

Patrick felt a flush of surprise mixed with terror, followed quickly by a surge of validation. It was Garrett acknowledging that he was more than just "Paris."

"Right," Patrick said, his voice steady. He pulled his shoulders back, stepping into the role. "Okay. Everyone, take your positions for the opening sequence. Let's clean up the spacing."

The morning turned into a grueling workshop. Patrick moved through the room, correcting posture, adjusting arms, and trying to teach a room full of actors how to count to eight. It felt good to be competent, to have a domain where he was the expert.

Between sequences, Patrick and Dean were increasingly attached at the hip. Some of it was practical, Patrick fixing Dean's stance, but some of it wasn't.

"All right, Romeo," Patrick said, walking over to Dean, who was trying to execute a turn without tripping. "Less giraffe, more gazelle. Or, honestly, less flailing. I believe in you."

Dean wrinkled his nose. "This feels like revenge for me making you recite Shakespeare in a broom closet."

Patrick chuckled and took Dean's hand, adjusting his grip. "Now, step here…spin…"

Dean did, not gracefully, but with enough earnestness that Patrick felt something swell in his chest. He didn't let go right away.

"You make it look effortless," Dean murmured, a little breathless, his eyes locked on Patrick's.

"That's the trick, Clarke. I'm dying inside."

Their hands lingered a beat too long before Patrick turned away.

"Okay!" Garrett called out, clapping his hands. "Let's run the meeting scene. The first touch. Romeo and Julius. Masks on."

The energy shifted immediately. Music pulsed through the space, classical with sudden streaks of modern synths, a Baz Luhrmann-esque collision of eras.

Jacob stepped forward, pulling on his mask. Dean did the same, the silver half-mask making his eyes look dangerous and bright.

They circled each other. They reached out.

And then Jacob tripped over his own feet, slamming into Dean's chest with the grace of a sack of potatoes.

"Hold!" Garrett yelled, rubbing his temples. "Jacob, you are mauling him. It is a dance of seduction, not a collision."

"I'm trying!" Jacob protested, red-faced. "The steps are weird! My feet don't do that!"

Garrett sighed, a sound of deep existential fatigue. "Patrick. Demonstrate."

Patrick froze. "Demonstrate?"

"Dance the Julius part with Dean so Jacob can see what it's supposed to look like."

The room went quiet. Patrick looked at Dean. Dean raised an eyebrow behind his mask, a challenge and an invitation in his eyes.

Dean stepped forward, offering his hand.

Patrick took it.

The contact was immediate and electric, a current that snapped from Dean's palm straight up Patrick's arm. Dean's hand was warm, his grip firm, his skin rougher than Patrick expected.

"Music!" Garrett barked.

The synth beat kicked in, a heavy, throbbing rhythm that seemed to vibrate in the floorboards. Patrick didn't have to think. He let the training take over, but the feeling... the feeling was something else entirely.

He moved into Dean's space, not tentatively, but with a terrifying kind of inevitability. The world outside the two of them dissolved into a meaningless blur.

There was only the heat radiating off Dean's body. The scent of him filled Patrick's senses, dizzying and grounding all at once.

Patrick spun away, the movement sharp, precise, before pulling back in, using the tension in their joined hands like a tether. He crashed back against Dean's chest, his back flush against the solid wall of Dean's front. He could feel Dean's heart hammering against his spine, matching the frantic rhythm of his own.

Then the tempo slowed. The moment of recognition.

Patrick turned in the circle of Dean's arms, looking up. Dean didn't step back. Instead, his hand slid up from Patrick's shoulder, his fingers threading through the hair at the nape of Patrick's neck before settling warm and firm against the side of his face.

It was a touch so tender, so startlingly intimate, that Patrick's breath hitched in his throat.

Without thinking, Patrick reached up. He covered Dean's hand with his own, pressing it closer, anchoring himself to the touch. Dean's thumb brushed his cheekbone, a feather-light caress.

They began to spin, slow and hypnotic.

Through the silver mask, Dean's eyes were dark, blown wide. They weren't looking at "Julius." They were looking at Patrick.

Patrick felt untethered, floating. It was an out-of-body experience, a lucid dream where gravity only existed where Dean touched him. He forgot the steps. He forgot he was demonstrating. He simply reacted.

They revolved in silence, a slow-motion orbit. The rest of the room fell away completely. There was only the warmth of Dean's palm against his cheek, the weight of Dean's gaze, and the overwhelming, terrifying realization that this wasn't acting.

Dean's gaze dropped to Patrick's mouth. Patrick saw the twitch of Dean's jaw, felt the ghost of a breath against his lips. The pull to close the gap was physical, a magnetic force that made his entire body ache.

"And...hold," Garrett said.

The voice came from a million miles away.

"That. That is what I want. The friction. Thank you, Patrick."

Patrick scrambled upright, stumbling slightly as reality came crashing back in. He stepped back, his skin burning where Dean had touched him, his lungs gasping for air that suddenly felt too thin.

He avoided looking at the rest of the cast. He felt exposed. Raw.

"Right," Patrick said, his voice cracking slightly. "Just...like that. Jacob."

Jacob snorted from the sidelines, arms crossed defensively. "Yeah, yeah. Very pretty. You guys practice that in your room last night?"

The spell broke.

Dean turned on his heel, his face darkening. "It's called professionalism, Jacob. Try it sometime."

Patrick busied himself with his water bottle, heart hammering a frantic rhythm against his ribs.

As Garrett called for a short break, Patrick slipped away, still catching his breath from the last sequence. The choreography had left his limbs buzzing and his thoughts tangled in the proximity of Dean's body, the accidental intimacy of dancing face to face, mask to mask.

Jess caught up to him near the side exit, two bottles of water in hand. She held one out wordlessly.

"Thanks," Patrick said, gratefully accepting it.

"You looked like you needed a breather," Jess said, bumping his shoulder lightly. "Or an exorcism. Hard to tell sometimes."

Patrick huffed out a laugh, but it faded quickly. "Yeah. Just…trying not to spiral."

"This about the dancing? Or the fact that you and Dean just undressed each other with your eyes in front of the entire cast?"

Patrick choked on his water. "We did not."

"Patrick, honey. The air conditioning kicked on and the room still got hotter. It was…intense."

Patrick looked away, leaning against the brick wall of the alleyway. "It's just acting, Jess. He's Romeo. I was just…demonstrating."

"Patrick, you can lie to Jacob, and you can maybe even lie to Garrett," Jess said gently, bumping his shoulder. "But don't lie to yourself. That wasn't acting. That was feeling. And that's okay."

He glanced at her. "Even if those feelings are maybe a little doomed? I'm Paris, Jess. I'm literally the obstacle."

"Especially then. What's a good love story without a little doom?" Jess grinned. "Besides, did you see Jacob's face? He looked like he wanted to sue you for emotional distress."

Patrick gave her a tired smile. "You're way too wise for someone who drinks three Red Bulls a day."

"Don't knock the process. Besides, someone's gotta keep you from spiraling out mid-rehearsal. Consider it my civic duty."

They wandered back toward the studio, laughter fading into thoughtful quiet. As they reached the main hallway, Jess peeled off toward the bathroom with a final, supportive wink.

Patrick stepped through the side door and into the corridor, just in time to hear Dean's voice.

He froze instinctively, ducking behind a column by the vending machines. Dean stood with his back to him, phone to his ear, his entire frame taut with tension.

"No, Mum, I am taking it seriously," Dean said, his voice low but strained. "You think I don't know what's riding on this? I'm trying. I just need you to—"

A pause. Then more quietly: "I know I'm not her. I never was."

Patrick's breath caught. *Her?*

"I didn't pick this to make a point," Dean went on. "I picked it because I finally found something I love. Because it feels like mine. And I'm not quitting."

Another pause. The silence on the other end stretched long. Dean's posture stiffened.

"Okay. I have to go."

He hung up quickly, the tension still radiating off him in waves.

Patrick shifted slightly, instinct urging him to step back, but Dean turned before he could.

Their eyes met. Patrick saw the flicker of something raw before Dean blinked it away.

"Hey. Just catching up with my mum," Dean said, clearing his throat, his voice returning to its usual warm register.

"You okay?" Patrick asked.

Dean's smile was too practiced, too quick. "'Course. Just family stuff."

"You don't have to pretend with me."

Dean looked at him then, really looked, his smile faltering just a bit. For a second the vulnerability Patrick had overheard hovered in his expression like a ghost.

Then Garrett's voice rang out from the rehearsal room, sharp and commanding: "Clarke! O'Connell! Back in!"

Dean stepped forward, the moment dissolving as he passed Patrick with a faint smile and a nudge to his arm.

"Come on! Time to dance like our lives depend on it."

And just like that, the mask was back.

There was more to Dean than charm and clever lines. And beneath the polished exterior, something very real was cracking through.

Back inside the studio, the rehearsal was heating up again.

Patrick and Dean fell back into step, their movements tighter now. Patrick still felt that echo of the phone call, humming just under the choreography. Dean wasn't talking about it, but the shadows under his eyes hadn't vanished.

They were mid-sequence, Patrick correcting Dean's hand placement for the fifth time, when Jacob slithered into their orbit like a misplaced stage direction.

"Well, well. If it isn't our very own Romeo and Paris. You are committing to the whole dance captain thing, huh?"

Patrick tensed instinctively, but Dean didn't miss a beat. He stepped slightly in front of Patrick, not overtly but enough to be noticed.

"Are you lost, Jacob?" Dean said, voice light but cool.

Jacob shrugged, that smirk of his coiled tight around every word. "Just observing. You know, learning from the masters. It's amazing how...close you two have gotten. Very authentic. Very...intimate."

His gaze lingered deliberately, trying to needle, to make something stick.

Patrick felt heat rise in his cheeks, but this time, it wasn't embarrassment. It was anger.

He opened his mouth, but Dean beat him to it.

"It's called chemistry, Jacob. Something directors like.

And audiences. You'd be amazed what happens when you actually focus on the work instead of the mirror."

Jacob's smile faltered for half a second, then hardened.

"Sure. Just remember not everyone's watching the same play," he said, then sauntered off, his retreat lacking its usual smug swagger.

Dean let out a breath and turned back to Patrick. "You okay?"

"Yeah. I just…I hate the way he tries to twist everything. Like it's all some big joke."

"He wants a reaction. Don't give him one," Dean said, his gaze softening.

"You didn't just not give him a reaction. You performed a reaction," Patrick said.

Dean smirked. "Well, we are in rehearsal."

Patrick let out a laugh, tension easing slightly. But something in his chest still buzzed—anger, yes, but also a strange, bittersweet awareness of how close everything was to unraveling. How quickly the boundary between acting and real feeling had blurred.

Jess jogged by and gave Patrick a look that said, "You good?" He nodded faintly.

"Back to one!" Garrett called, voice echoing off the walls. "Let's take it from the entrance. This time, with energy!"

As they moved back to their places, Patrick glanced once more at Dean. He still wore the same practiced smile.

But now Patrick knew what might lie beneath it.

CHAPTER 11

On a rare, sun-drenched afternoon, a blessed reprieve from the relentless RADA schedule, Patrick and Dean slipped free of Schaffer House and rehearsals and let London carry them toward Regent's Park. The decision hadn't been planned, exactly. But Patrick had seen it coming. For days he'd watched Dean fray around the edges—taking more moments to himself in empty corridors, pacing while on hushed phone calls, his eyes tight with an anxiety that didn't match his usual easy charm. The cracks were showing, and today, after a rehearsal where Dean looked like he was vibrating with exhaustion, Patrick had simply decided enough was enough.

Regent's Park unfolded like another country altogether, a vast green lung in the middle of the city. It felt like stepping through a secret door, one moment bus exhaust and shouting cyclists, the next, sunlight pouring through ancient trees, the smell of roses in the air, the air softer somehow. Joggers passed with rhythmic footfalls and children's shrieks of laughter tangled with the faint strains of a busker's violin. Somewhere, a vendor was roasting peanuts, the scent drifting like smoke.

Patrick couldn't remember the last time he'd felt such space around him. The rehearsals, the deadlines, the constant pressure of Garrett's gaze, all of it felt temporarily suspended, left behind at the park gates.

They found their spot beneath a broad oak tree whose branches arched like cathedral rafters. The grass there was lush and cool, patchy with sunlight. Dean unfurled a blanket in ridiculous stripes of turquoise and orange, plopped his bag down, and dropped onto it with a theatrical sigh. Patrick followed, stretching out, feeling the ground solid under his back.

The quiet wasn't silence; it was layered, textured. The wind through leaves. The squeak of a swing somewhere far off. Snippets of conversation carried on the breeze, "*...and then she said she'd never even heard of Pinter!*"

"*...no, the dog's fine, just ate the tulips again...*"

Patrick smiled faintly, letting it wash over him. For the first time in weeks, his body unclenched.

"Right. Today's lesson in British culture: essential summer tunes. Consider it your immersion. You can't understand the British soul without its soundtrack. It's like trying to do Shakespeare without the iambic pentameter, possible, but soulless," Dean said, tugging his phone from his pocket and holding it like a conductor's baton, grin full of mischief.

"Do I need to take notes?" Patrick chuckled.

Dean tapped a few times. A wistful guitar riff drifted into the air, followed by a voice both plaintive and raw: *"Dirty old river…"*

Patrick blinked. He had never heard it before, but something in those first notes snagged him, timeless, melancholy, like opening an old family album full of strangers' faces and feeling their lives anyway.

"The Kinks. 'Waterloo Sunset.' Quintessential London," Dean said, his grin softening.

"It feels nostalgic. Like remembering a life you never lived. Like the city itself is sighing," Patrick said, leaning back on his elbows, eyes closing to let the song sink in.

"Exactly. It's about finding beauty in the everyday. That fleeting magic. It's our song, I think. For this summer. For us." Dean's voice was quiet now, almost reverent.

He said it casually, as though it meant nothing, but Patrick felt it like a stone dropped into deep water, a ripple expanding, touching everything inside him. His pulse jumped. He turned his head, caught the sunlight in Dean's hair, the auburn sparks among the darker strands, and wanted to say something, but the words clung stubbornly to his tongue.

They traded songs, volleying back and forth until the blanket felt like the center of their own private universe.

Patrick offered his favorite American indie bands, all obscure names and aching lyrics, while Dean countered with classics, pulling out Bowie, The Beatles, a guilty-pleasure Blur anthem. Patrick, in turn, insisted on playing Gaga, rolling his eyes at Dean's mock groans while defending her as "the closest thing our generation has to Shakespeare with a disco stick." He even slipped in his love for John Williams, making Dean endure the *Jurassic Park* theme echoing through the trees.

"You're unbelievable," Dean laughed, shaking his head as the orchestra swelled.

"And you're uncultured," Patrick shot back with a grin.

Each choice was like a breadcrumb, revealing something of who they were when the costumes came off.

At some point, Dean leaned into his bag and pulled out two sweating bottles of Old Mout Cider, holding them up like a conjurer's prize.

"You came prepared," Patrick laughed, delighted.

"Obviously. It's practically illegal to spend a summer's day outdoors without one. Tradition," Dean said, twisting the cap off with mock ceremony.

The cider was crisp and fruity, fizz sharp on Patrick's tongue. The glass sweated in his hand, droplets trailing over his fingers and dampening the grass. The alcohol threaded through him with warmth, loosening the last tight corners of his body. He stretched long, arms overhead, feeling like the sun itself was soaking into him.

Something in him sparked, a little reckless, a little joyful. He stood abruptly and let the music tug him into movement. Not choreographed, not for performance. Just spinning, loose-limbed, clumsy, alive. The world narrowed to grass underfoot, the sky wheeling overhead, his body surrendering to rhythm.

When he stumbled to a stop, breathless and flushed, Dean was watching him from the blanket. Not laughing. Not mocking. Watching with that steady, unblinking intensity that made Patrick feel both exposed and held.

Then Dean reached into his bag again and produced a battered Canon AE-1. The soft click of the shutter cut through the music. Another. And another.

"Seriously?" Patrick laughed, swiping hair from his face.

"Keep going," Dean said, lowering the camera just enough to grin.

Another click. Another frozen second. And Patrick realized with a thrum of awareness that it wasn't about photographs. It was about being seen.

Breathless, Patrick collapsed back onto the blanket, limbs splayed inelegantly, chest rising and falling in quick bursts. He could still feel the sun's heat on his skin, the grass pressed into the back of his shirt, the fizz of cider humming through his veins.

"Got it. The definitive portrait of a man possessed," Dean grinned, lowering the camera.

"Delete them. All of them. Burn the negatives. Scatter the ashes in the Thames," Patrick groaned, covering his face with an arm.

"Absolutely not. I'll develop them myself. Exhibit A in *Why Patrick Should Never Doubt His Own Charm*," Dean said, peering through the lens once more before setting the camera aside.

Patrick peeked at him from under his arm, rolling his eyes but feeling something warm and dangerous expand in his chest. "Alright, your turn then, Mr. Photographer. Let's see you dance. Or are you afraid your brooding intensity will terrify the pelicans into a synchronized retreat?"

"I'll spare the wildlife. Besides, you're the graceful one. I'm better behind the lens, capturing magic, not making it," Dean chuckled, flopping back beside him.

Patrick nudged his foot against Dean's in mock reproach, though secretly relieved. Part of him had wanted to see Dean stumble awkwardly across the grass; another part feared that if Dean had danced, Patrick's chest might have actually combusted.

The cider bottles clinked softly between them as Dean shifted onto his side, propping himself up on one elbow. The sunlight fell across his face, catching in his hair, tracing gold across his jaw. For a long moment, Dean just looked at him—no smirk, no quip, only quiet consideration.

Patrick swallowed and looked away, picking at the damp label on his cider bottle. His pulse was suddenly too loud in his ears.

Dean reached for the *Romeo and Julius* script they'd abandoned under the pile of clothes and waved it with mock severity. "Right. Duty calls. Garrett's already sharpening his knives for me. If I can't die convincingly by Monday, he'll murder me for real."

Patrick grinned, thumbing through pages until he found the balcony scene. They began, voices soft at first, reciting familiar lines into the canopy of leaves above them. But it wasn't long before Patrick's mischievous streak took over.

"Oh, Dean, Dean! Wherefore art thou, Dean?" Patrick cried in mock anguish, jabbing the script into his ribs.

Before he could gloat further, Dean lunged, fingers digging mercilessly into his sides. Patrick shrieked, twisting and flailing, laughter bursting uncontrollably from his chest. The script went flying, landing somewhere in the grass as they collapsed into a heap, limbs tangled, laughter shaking them both.

"Mercy! I yield! Traitorous villain," Patrick gasped, helpless with laughter.

Dean only tickled harder, until Patrick rolled onto his back, breathless and red-faced, eyes streaming with tears.

Then, without quite meaning to, Patrick ended up sprawled half on top of him, his head pressing into Dean's chest, the steady thump of his heartbeat grounding and dizzying all at once. The laughter faded into breathless silence. Dean's arm slipped around him instinctively, not tight but certain. A quiet, unconscious claim.

Patrick stilled, cheek pressed to the rise and fall of Dean's chest. His breath was still uneven but not from laughter anymore. The warmth beneath him was steady, real, and terrifying in its simplicity. He could hear Dean's heartbeat, unhurried yet strong, and it felt like it echoed through his own ribcage, syncing with his pulse until he couldn't tell which belonged to whom.

The sunlight slanted through the oak branches above, flickering in and out like a film reel. Every time the light touched Dean's face, Patrick felt his throat tighten. He had spent countless hours watching him in rehearsals, in dorm corridors, under the dim cafeteria lights. But here, outside, in the unapologetic honesty of daylight, Dean was arresting. His lashes cast faint shadows against his cheek. The edges of his hair glowed auburn, like embers hidden in dark strands. His lips curved into the ghost of a smile, soft and unguarded, as though the world wasn't watching.

Patrick wanted to memorize it. To bottle this exact moment, to develop it like one of Dean's photographs, edges crisp and eternal. He imagined pulling it out years later: *Here. This is the afternoon when I almost told him.*

The words pressed against his teeth, insistent. He could feel them crowding, dangerous and inevitable. *I like you. More than I should. More than I've ever liked anyone.*

The thought of saying it aloud felt like stepping off a

cliff. What if it broke the moment? What if it shattered everything fragile and good between them? Fear coiled sharp in his chest, holding him back.

So instead, he swallowed it down, forcing a shaky laugh into the silence. The air smelled of grass and cider and the faint tang of Dean's cologne, and Patrick told himself it was enough. For now. To lie here, to listen to that heartbeat, to let the afternoon stretch golden and endless around them.

The speaker on Dean's phone crackled back into life, "Waterloo Sunset" lilting once more, and Patrick thought fleetingly: *If this is a dream, let me never wake up.*

They didn't move for a long while. The only sounds were the rustle of leaves overhead and the faint, looping guitar from Dean's speaker. Patrick focused on the steady thud of Dean's heart under his ear. It should have been grounding; instead, it made his pulse race, his body hyperaware of every place they touched.

"Careful. Keep this up, and I'll start expecting cuddles every rehearsal break," Patrick said, forcing a crooked smile.

"Don't tempt me. Garrett might start charging us extra for intimacy training," Dean laughed, the sound rumbling through Patrick's cheek where it rested against him.

Patrick laughed too, though it came out thinner, more breathless. He tilted his head up, just slightly, enough to catch Dean's gaze. For a second, their eyes locked, and the world stilled. Dean's smile softened, less of the practiced charm—more raw, something quieter underneath.

Dean looked away first, eyes tracing the shifting mosaic of oak leaves above them. Still Patrick felt the charge linger between them, humming like static. *It feels like something out of a film,* Patrick thought. Like those afternoons in *Call Me By Your Name*, the lazy golden light, the weight of unspoken possibility.

"You know," Dean said softly, breaking the silence, his eyes still fixed on the leaves. "You have this natural grace. Even when you're just messing around. When did you start? Dancing, I mean."

Patrick blinked, surprised by the question. He hesitated, tracing a pattern on the blanket. "Sixteen."

Dean's eyebrows shot up. "Sixteen? Christ, that's practically geriatric for a dancer, isn't it?"

Patrick laughed dryly. "Tell me about it. I was way behind. But starting late wasn't actually the hard part. It was the silence."

"The silence?"

Patrick nodded, a bitter smile touching his lips. "With my dad. It was never about who I loved. The real war was about ballet. When I told him I wanted to do this professionally... it was just months of dead air. Dismissive questions about when I'd get a 'real job.' That silence... It drove me to prove my worth every single day. To show him I wasn't wasting my life."

He looked up, meeting Dean's gaze. "That's why I came here. To prove I could be more than just a dancer. To prove I had something else to say."

Dean listened intently, his expression softening into something fierce and protective. "Well, Patrick O'Connell. You should be so proud of yourself," he said firmly. "You've accomplished so much already. You don't need to prove anything to him. Or anyone."

Patrick felt a lump form in his throat at the certainty in Dean's voice. "Thanks, Dean."

He took a breath, feeling the air clearer between them now. The vulnerability felt like an open door, a permission slip.

"So…" Patrick started carefully. "Is that what it is with you? With your parents?"

Dean went still.

"That phone call the other day," Patrick pressed gently. "And lately…you've been disappearing. Looking like you're carrying the weight of the world. Is it like my dad? Are they pressuring you?"

Dean's jaw flexed. For a moment, he looked like he might deflect, toss out some easy quip. But then his shoulders slumped, the practiced ease slipping.

"She doesn't get it. My mum. My dad either. It's not just that they don't think much of acting. It's…they're scared of it."

Dean sat up abruptly, as if he couldn't bear to be lying

down anymore. The sudden movement dislodged Patrick, who sat up with him, crossing his legs and leaning in close.

Dean stared out at the park, at the families and the dogs, his hands gripping his knees.

"My sister. Emilia," Dean said, his voice brittle. "She was the actor. She was the one with the spark. I was just the little brother who tagged along to carry her bags. She was brilliant, Patrick."

Patrick went still.

"Two years ago," Dean continued, his voice wavering now. "She was driving back from a rehearsal. It was late. Raining. She was exhausted from the schedule."

He stopped, taking a jagged breath.

"She fell asleep at the wheel and hit a barrier. She died instantly."

A tear slipped down Dean's cheek. He angrily wiped it away, but another followed.

"They look at me, Patrick, and they don't see me following a dream. They see me doing the exact thing that killed her. The late nights. The exhaustion. The obsession. To them, the acting isn't art. It's the thing that took their daughter."

Dean's voice broke completely, a sob catching in his throat.

"I'm terrified," he whispered, tears now falling freely. "I feel like I have to be good enough for both of us. Like if I fail, I'm letting her down. But if I succeed... I'm losing my parents."

Patrick didn't hesitate. He reached out, taking Dean's face in his hands, guiding him in until Dean's forehead rested against his chest. Patrick wrapped his arms around him, holding him tight as Dean finally let go, his shoulders shaking.

"It's okay," Patrick murmured into Dean's hair, rubbing slow, soothing circles on his back. "It's okay, Dean. You've all gone through so much. You're allowed to be scared."

Dean gripped Patrick's shirt, holding on like a lifeline.

"I'm sure Emilia would be so proud of you," Patrick whispered.

Dean let out a shuddering breath against Patrick's chest, the tension slowly draining out of him.

"Thank you," Dean choked out, his voice muffled.

Patrick just held him tighter.

"I'm always going to be here for you," Patrick whispered against his temple. "You're going to get through this."

He pressed his cheek to the top of Dean's head and listened to the steady rhythm of his breathing return.

After a moment, Patrick gently guided them both backward, lowering them until they were sprawled on the blanket once more. He pulled Dean close, draping an arm around him as they stared up at the sky, letting the music wash over them while the sun set around them.

CHAPTER 12

July 22nd arrived with a London sunrise so obnoxiously cheerful it felt like a personal attack. Patrick's phone buzzed violently against the nightstand, vibrating with the determination of a toddler on a sugar high. He groaned, reached blindly, and squinted at the screen.

It was the group chat with LaShelle and Eli.

LaShelle: *happy birthday, patrick!! you better be living it up in london! 27 looks good on you!*

Eli: *hope they've got proper birthday cake over there and not just crumpets and despair. you deserve the world, p-man.*

LaShelle: *we love you! don't let anyone ruin your night!*

Patrick smiled despite himself, warmth rising like champagne bubbles. He typed back quickly.

Patrick: *thanks, you two! miss you so much. london's got my back. about to head to a pub with the hot british guy i'm* definitely *not falling for.*

A pause. Then the inevitable onslaught:

Eli: *!!!*

LaShelle: *HELP IS ON THE WAY DEAR!!*

Eli: *spill. the. tea.*

Patrick laughed out loud, the sound too bright, too giddy for 9 AM. His neighbors could deal with it. He closed the chat before the interrogation escalated into a full digital inquisition, his heart still buzzing.

Almost immediately another notification lit up his phone. A group chat from his mom, Aunt Therese, Aunt Ann.

Mom: *Happy Birthday, sweetheart! Love you so much. Can't believe my baby is 27!*

Aunt Therese: *Happy Birthday, darling boy!! I hope you're eating cake for breakfast.*

Aunt Ann: *Happy birthday, sweetheart. We're so proud of you…sending the biggest hug across the   ocean!*

Patrick snorted softly, his chest aching in the best way. He thumbed back a reply.

Patrick: *Thanks, you three. Don't worry, I'll keep my questionable decisions to a minimum.*

He dropped the phone on his chest and let out a long breath. A year older, allegedly wiser, and definitely more tangled up in Dean than he had any business being. And tonight, a salsa club, a birthday, the whole gang showing up. Including Olivia. Including the stage-kiss-shaped elephant in the room.

Later that afternoon, Patrick ducked into The Marlborough Arms with Jess. The pub smelled of varnished oak and history, the kind of place where time stuck to the beams like cigarette smoke. Jess slid into their corner booth with a practiced ease, already halfway through ordering drinks by the time Patrick sat down.

"Happy birthday, Broadway. One more year wiser, infinitely more dramatic," Jess said, pushing a pint across to him and raising her own glass in salute.

"To being dramatic. May my death rattles always bring Garrett to tears," Patrick said, clinking her glass with exaggerated solemnity.

"Honestly, you're already halfway there. That man doesn't know what to do with you. Which makes me love you more," Jess laughed, a sharp, melodic sound that turned a few heads.

"You're just saying that because you're in love with Monty and don't want me stealing the spotlight," Patrick said, leaning back with a grin as he took a sip.

"Excuse you. Monty is—" Jess made a face, her cheeks coloring just slightly, an uncharacteristic tell. She waved a hand vaguely, as if gesturing could substitute for words. "He's fun. Don't make it weird."

"Fun, right. Sure. Not at all can't-stop-smiling-when-he-texts-you fun. Not at all 'wirls-his-hair-like-a-romcom-heroine fun. Totally platonic fun," Patrick smirked.

"I hate you," Jess said, throwing a peanut at his forehead.

"You love me," Patrick said, ducking the second

peanut and grinning. Then, softer: "He's good for you. I can see it. Makes you lighter."

"Fine. Maybe I like him. Just a little. Don't tell him. Or I'll murder you on your birthday," Jess said, rolling her eyes but unable to stop the corner of her mouth from curling up.

"You deserve someone who sees you the way you want to be seen. Nothing less," Patrick said, leaning forward, chin propped on his hand, his grin now less teasing, more wistful.

"You're projecting," Jess said, tilting her head and studying him.

"Maybe," Patrick said, his smile faltering as he reached for his pint, buying himself a moment.

"So. Dean," Jess said, her voice softening.

"Ugh, must we?" Patrick said, letting out a dramatic groan and slumping against the booth.

"Yes. We must," Jess smirked, merciless.

"It's…bad, Jess. Like, head-over-heels, can't-breathe bad. Every time he looks at me, it feels like someone switched the world into HD. And don't you dare quote that in your screenplay later," Patrick said, peaking at her through his lashes, caught between confession and denial until the words spilled anyway.

"To Dean. The hot British guy currently making Patrick O'Connell completely unhinged," Jess said, lifting her pint in mock solemnity.

"Tragic, isn't it?" Patrick said, clinking his glass against hers with a sigh, trying not to smile.

"You're glowing, darling," Jess said.

Patrick rolled his eyes skyward, but his chest buzzed with something close to hope.

After Jess finished psychoanalyzing his love life, and threatening to murder him if he told Monty anything, Patrick escaped the pub with equal parts mortification and giddiness. Back at Schaffer House, his room looked like the aftermath of a tornado in Zara.

Patrick's dorm room at Schaffer House was a whirlwind of nervous energy and discarded clothes. He was trying to decide on the perfect outfit for the salsa club, something that said *effortlessly cool dancer* and not *desperate American trying too hard*.

He started to rummage through his suitcase when his fingers brushed against soft velvet. He paused.

He pulled out the small black pouch he had buried at the bottom of his bag. Inside were the two silver compass necklaces he purchased for himself and Victor.

Patrick tipped the pouch, letting one of the compasses slide into his palm. The silver caught the light. He thought about putting it back, saving it for a "right" time that would never come.

No, he thought, a sudden surge of defiance rising in his chest.

He unclasped the chain and fastened it around his own

neck. It settled against his collarbone, cool and grounding. A reminder to follow his own direction.

He had just pulled off his jeans, standing in his boxer briefs, debating between a black button-down and a slightly less formal patterned shirt, when there was a soft knock on his open door.

"Patrick? You decent, mate?" Dean's voice, warm and familiar, drifted in.

"Come in!" Patrick called out, a flush rising on his cheeks, a sudden self-consciousness washing over him. He quickly grabbed the patterned shirt, holding it strategically in front of him. "Just getting ready. I'll be ready in a second. Just have to change my pants."

Dean stepped into the room, looking impossibly handsome in a dark button-down shirt that made his hazel eyes seem even darker, like pools of melted chocolate. He carried a bright, helium-filled balloon that bobbed cheerfully above his head, an absurdly joyful counterpoint to his brooding aesthetic, and a small, thoughtfully wrapped gift bag.

"Happy birthday, Patrick." His smile was warm and genuine, his eyes crinkling at the corners. "You always look handsome, but tonight you look particularly dashing. Ready to set the dance floor on fire?"

With a playful grin, Dean launched himself onto Patrick's bed, propping himself up on his elbows as he watched Patrick in the mirror, who was meticulously adjusting his cuff links.

Dean's gaze drifted, casually at first, then lingered, sweeping down Patrick's exposed legs. Patrick felt a sudden, intense awareness of his body, the dancer's physique he usually took for granted. He saw Dean's eyes widen almost imperceptibly, a flicker of surprise, then something deeper, something intensely appreciative, pass through them.

"Holy shit," Dean murmured, his voice low, almost reverent, a hint of genuine awe in his tone. His gaze was fixed on Patrick's legs, then his glutes, a slow, deliberate appraisal. "Your legs are…incredibly fit. And your arse, mate. Damn."

A playful yet undeniably admiring smirk touched his lips, and his eyes, now sparkling with a new kind of mischief, met Patrick's.

Patrick's cheeks flushed a deep crimson, a full-body blush that had nothing to do with the summer heat and everything to do with Dean's direct, unabashed admiration. He felt a jolt, a delicious thrill that shot straight through him, a mixture of embarrassment and profound, unexpected pleasure.

He quickly pulled on his pants, trying to hide the sudden flutter in his stomach, the frantic beating of his heart. "That would be the ballet, dear." He added a playful wink, his mock indignation barely concealing his delight.

Dean chuckled, a warm, resonant sound that filled the

small room. "Well, it's certainly paying off, isn't it? Just stating facts, O'Connell. Purely artistic appreciation. A dancer's physique is a work of art, after all. And yours, in particular, is…quite a masterpiece."

He dropped the balloon, letting it float to the ceiling, and sat casually on the edge of Patrick's bed, leaning back on his hands, his gaze still holding Patrick's, a silent invitation to acknowledge the charged moment.

"Here. Before we get too distracted," Dean said.

Patrick took the bag, peering inside. He pulled out a small box, and inside sat a detailed figurine of Yoda.

Patrick burst out laughing. "You did not."

"It's so we can remember that was our first movie together," Dean said, grinning.

Dean leaned back on his hands, looking amused. "Consider it a peace offering. I need to keep my allies close. I didn't realize I'd be the token Brit in a group full of Americans this summer. I'm practically outnumbered. It's been...entertaining."

"I love him," Patrick said, genuinely touched. He set the figure on his nightstand. "Thank you, Dean. And don't worry, we're very friendly invaders."

As he turned back, Dean's eyes caught the silver glint at Patrick's throat. He leaned forward slightly.

"That's new," Dean said, nodding at the compass. "I haven't seen you wear that before. It's beautiful."

Patrick's hand went instinctively to the compass

pendant. He felt the cool metal under his thumb.

"Oh, this?" Patrick said, keeping his voice light, waving a hand dismissively. "Just something I bought in New York ages ago. Found it at the bottom of my bag and thought, why not?"

Dean studied him for a second, as if sensing there was more to the story, but he didn't push.

"Thanks for coming, Dean." Patrick's voice was still a little shaky, trying to regain some semblance of normalcy.

"My pleasure, Patrick." Dean stood up, smoothing his shirt. "Now, are you ready to set the dance, or are you going to stand there contemplating the profound implications of your sartorial choices all night?"

Patrick grabbed his shoes, rolling his eyes with theatrical flair. "Careful, or I'll make you lead the first salsa number. See how philosophical you get then."

"Tragic," Dean said with mock seriousness, hopping off the bed to straighten his cuffs. "I'd be forced to retire in disgrace after stepping on every poor soul's toes."

"You'd love the attention," Patrick said, slipping into his jacket and smoothing the fabric down with unnecessary precision. "Headline news: RADA's broodiest star falls victim to rhythm. More at eleven."

Dean grinned, leaning against the doorframe. "You'd still make me look good."

Patrick froze just long enough to feel it, the way Dean's words slipped past casual and landed somewhere heavier.

He cleared his throat, tugging unnecessarily at his collar. "Flattery will not save you from my choreography, dear."

"Worth a try," Dean said, laughter warm in his voice. He gestured toward the hall. "Come on then, birthday boy. Everyone's waiting. Let's make an entrance."

The common room at Schaffer House buzzed with pre-party energy. Music thumped faintly from someone's speaker, and the air smelled of hairspray, aftershave, and nervous excitement. Patrick and Dean stepped in together, and for one ridiculous second, Patrick imagined them as some kind of power couple making a red-carpet entrance.

"Finally!" Monty called from the couch, already halfway through a cider. "Birthday royalty has arrived. Took you long enough. Jess was about to start a manhunt."

Jess, perched on the arm of the chair beside him, smirked. "Please. I'd have found him in two minutes flat. Patrick leaves a trail of drama wherever he goes."

Patrick swept into a mock bow, hand over his heart. "Guilty as charged. Theatrical chaos is my brand."

"Your brand and your downfall," Jess shot back, though the corner of her mouth twitched into a grin.

Around them, the rest of the cohorts trickled in: Fortune, Swan, Lysander, Rose, Perdita. The whole mad Romeo and Julius circus had somehow been corralled into one room, everyone decked out in some attempt at "salsa chic." The energy was infectious, laughter spilling over the edges of every conversation.

Dean handed Patrick a cider, their fingers brushing in a way that made Patrick's chest buzz. "To your health, birthday boy. May tonight bring you both rhythm and questionable life choices."

Patrick clinked his bottle against Dean's with a wry smile. "One out of two is inevitable."

The group erupted into chatter again, plans being made, jokes flying. For a fleeting moment, Patrick looked around the room and felt something sharp and sweet twist inside him. This was it—London, RADA, new friends who already felt like family. Dean at his side. His chest ached with a kind of joy he didn't know how to hold.

The trek from Schaffer House to the salsa club felt like its own parade. A gaggle of theater students heading to Soho was not exactly subtle. Patrick suspected they looked like a traveling circus powered by cheap cider and eyeliner. Someone had brought along a portable speaker, blasting Gloria Estefan, and Monty kept shouting, "The rhythm is gonna get you!" at startled passersby.

By the time they spilled into the club, the night was already humming. The air was thick with bass and sweat, colored lights flickering like a kaleidoscope. Couples twirled and dipped on the dance floor, their bodies moving in fast, joyful chaos, while clusters of people gathered around the bar, shouting to be heard over the music.

Patrick hesitated for a half-second at the threshold, taking it all in, the swirl of color, the pulse of music, the crush of bodies. He loved it instantly. This was his element, the sweet spot where performance and pleasure collided.

Dean leaned in close, his breath warm against Patrick's ear. "Ready to show London what Broadway looks like on tequila?"

Patrick grinned, the sound of Dean's voice practically vibrating down his spine. "Darling, I was born ready."

Jess snorted behind them. "Oh God, he's going to own the floor, and never let us forget it."

Monty clapped Patrick on the back. "As if he ever lets us forget anything."

They pushed deeper into the club, the crowd swallowing them whole. At the bar, Patrick ordered the first round, tequila shots lined up like soldiers, their rims glittering with salt.

"Happy birthday, Patrick!" someone yelled, raising their glass, and the cheer caught on, a ragged chorus of voices from their classmates echoing over the music. Patrick threw his back, the tequila burning hot and fast down his throat.

And then the music grabbed him. He didn't even think, just pulled Jess onto the dance floor, spinning her with a flourish that made her laugh so hard she nearly tripped. Monty whooped and jumped in, then half of Fortune followed until the floor was a frenzy of familiar faces and flailing limbs.

Patrick's body found its rhythm easily, years of ballet

making every turn sharp, every sway effortless. He let himself go, losing the weight of expectations, of auditions and critiques, of everything but the heat of the moment.

He glanced back toward the bar and found Dean watching him. Not drinking, not talking, just watching, that steady, consuming gaze that made Patrick's heart stumble.

Dean lifted his bottle in a tiny, private salute.

Patrick laughed, his pulse skipping. For one wild second, he thought: *Maybe tonight really will change everything.*

The night stretched into a blur of bodies and music. Patrick danced with anyone who grabbed his hand, Jess, Monty, even a grinning girl from Rose who kept trying to dip him until they both collapsed in laughter. Sweat slicked his neck, the tequila buzz thrummed pleasantly in his veins, and for the first time in weeks, he felt weightless.

"Show-off," Jess mouthed, but her grin was pure pride.

After a string of dances, Patrick finally begged off, laughing and breathless, and slipped toward the bar for water. His shirt clung damp to his back, his hair sticking up in wild tufts. He leaned against the counter, catching his breath, watching the crowd surge and spin like some sweaty, neon-tinted ocean.

That was when Jacob appeared.

He stumbled up, elbow knocking against Patrick's as if they were old mates instead of reluctant classmates. His grin was lopsided, his words slurring into each other. "Christ, O'Connell. You look good out there."

Patrick chuckled politely, already flagging the bartender. "Thanks. Years of practice. Mostly weddings and the occasional flash mob."

Jacob leaned closer, the sour stench of lager hitting Patrick square in the face. His voice dropped, clumsy but pointed. "You know…I'm straight. But I've had fun with guys before. Could with you if you'd like. Bet you'd be a good time."

His clammy hand clamped onto Patrick's arm.

Patrick stiffened, the familiar cocktail of irritation and disgust spiking hot in his chest. He opened his mouth, half to laugh it off, half to eviscerate Jacob with a perfectly timed one-liner, but he didn't get the chance.

Dean was suddenly there.

He pried Jacob's hand off Patrick with deliberate force, his touch protective but firm. His eyes were hard, his jaw set like stone.

"Alright, Jacob," Dean said, his voice low, flat, dangerous. "That's enough. Now fuck off."

The words cut sharper than the bass thundering through the speakers.

Jacob barked a drunken laugh, puffing himself up. "Oh, big man, yeah? What—is he your boyfriend now? Bit possessive, aren't you?"

Dean and Patrick exchanged a look that said if this were Hitchcock's Rope, Jacob would already be in the trunk.

Dean took a step closer, the air between them suddenly electric. His voice dropped to a near growl. "I said fuck. Off. Before I make you regret laying a finger on him. Don't you ever touch him again."

The shift was instant. Jacob's bravado faltered, his smirk collapsing under the weight of Dean's glare. He muttered something incoherent and slunk back into the crowd, shoulders hunched.

Patrick let out a shaky breath he hadn't realized he was holding. His pulse thundered in his ears.

Dean turned to him immediately, the steel in his expression melting into concern. His hand brushed Patrick's arm, gentle now. "You alright? Did he hurt you?"

Patrick swallowed hard, forcing a shaky laugh. "Only my faith in humanity. But otherwise, intact."

Dean gave a short, humorless laugh, shaking his head. "He's a fucking prick. Forget him. Come on, let's get back to the floor. Can't have your birthday ruined by some wanker with grabby hands."

He squeezed Patrick's hand before tugging him back toward the music, and Patrick let himself be pulled, still buzzing with adrenaline, and something else entirely.

He took Patrick's hand, his fingers warm and firm, and pulled him onto a less crowded part of the dance floor, leading him away from the lingering awkwardness, into the pulsating heart of the music.

Suddenly, the live percussion faded. The atmosphere

in the club shifted as a heavy, synthesized bass beat took over. The DJ was starting his set.

A familiar, electrifying string intro cut through the noise, and the crowd roared.

It was a remix of ABBA's "Gimme! Gimme! Gimme!"

Patrick laughed, throwing his head back as the pulse of the song vibrated through the floorboards.

He felt a body press against his back. Solid. Warm.

Hands slid onto his hips—firm, possessive thumbs digging into his waist.

Patrick gasped, his eyes flying open. He didn't need to turn around to know who it was.

Dean was right behind him, chest pressed flush against Patrick's back. He wasn't doing the polite "friends dancing" sway. He was grinding, slow and deliberate, matching Patrick's rhythm. He pulled Patrick closer, his grip tightening on Patrick's hips.

Patrick leaned back into the touch, his head falling back against Dean's shoulder, his heart hammering a frantic rhythm against his ribs. It felt electric.

But as quickly as the high came, the song transitioned.

The upbeat disco dissolved into a dark, throbbing synth line.

"Sweet dreams are made of this…"

A heavy remix of the Eurythmics filled the room.

Patrick laughed, spinning around in the crowd to face

Dean. "Did this DJ steal my playlist? This is literally my—
"

He stopped.

Dean wasn't there.

Patrick blinked, spinning in a circle. The crowd was a wall of bodies.

The strobe lights were flashing slowly now, slicing the room into disjointed, freezing frames. It was hard to make anyone out in the chaos.

Then, a flash of white light cut through the dark, and Patrick saw Dean near the edge of the dance floor.

He then saw Olivia reaching out, pulling Dean toward her.

Another strobe flash. Dean was standing close to her now, their faces illuminated in the stark, flickering light.

And then, Dean leaned in and kissed her.

It wasn't a clumsy peck. It was a lingering kiss, soft and deliberate, Olivia's hand rising to cup his cheek as though she'd done it a thousand times. Dean's arm slipped around her waist, pulling her close, possessive and easy in a way that shattered something inside Patrick.

Dean pulled back slightly, his hand still on Olivia's waist. He lifted his head.

And then, across the crowded floor, he looked straight at Patrick.

The strobe light froze them there: Dean's eyes wide, realizing too late who was watching. The look on his face matched the devastation on Patrick's.

Patrick's breath hitched, a sharp gasp that lodged in his throat. The music dulled to a low roar, the colors of the club fading into a smeared blur.

It was undeniable.

His chest caved in. The joy of the night, the fragile, shimmering hope he'd dared to let himself feel, crumbled in an instant. The betrayal was sharp and searing, a wound ripped open where he was already tender.

Tears stung his eyes before he could stop them. The air in the club suddenly felt too thick, too hot. The walls were closing in.

He couldn't breathe.

Panic clawed at his throat. He had to get out.

He turned and shoved his way through the throng of dancers, but the crowd felt like quicksand. Bodies bumped against him, sweaty and suffocating.

"Patrick! Pat!" someone yelled—maybe Monty, maybe Jess—but the sound warped underwater, unintelligible over the roaring in his ears.

He clutched at his shirt, his chest heaving as he gasped for air that wouldn't come. He pushed harder, desperate, a wild animal trying to escape a cage.

No one noticed him slipping under, just one more body vanishing into the night.

London's cool air hit him like a slap. The silence outside was brutal, the thumping bass replaced by the sound of his ragged breaths. Tears spilled freely now, streaking down his cheeks, blurring the streetlights into watery halos.

He walked blindly, first aimless, then desperate, his feet dragging him back toward Schaffer House as though pulled by gravity.

By the time he stumbled into his room, the last pieces of his birthday joy had splintered into dust. He collapsed onto the bed, curling into himself, his body wracked with sobs he couldn't contain.

His phone buzzed on the nightstand. With shaking hands, he picked it up.

A text:

Dean: *Patrick, please let me know where you are. I'm worried. Please just text me back.*

Patrick stared at the screen, the words swimming through the blur of his tears. The concern read like mockery, cruel in its timing.

He wanted to respond. He wanted to scream. He wanted to throw the phone against the wall.

But he was too exhausted, too broken.

The phone slipped from his grasp, landing on the duvet with a dull thud.

Patrick closed his eyes; the image of Dean kissing Olivia burned into his mind, searing and permanent.

And he fell asleep crying, the unanswered text glowing on the bedside table, a silent echo of everything he'd lost before it had even begun.

CHAPTER 13

Patrick woke to the shrill vibration of his phone rattling on the nightstand. His eyes cracked open against the watery light of morning, head pounding, chest still sore from the night before. The screen glowed with missed calls and a flood of messages:

Dean: *Where did you go? Are you alright? Patrick. Please answer.*

Jess: *Pat, seriously, what happened? You disappeared. Text me when you wake up.*

Monty: *Dude, please tell me you didn't end up in a ditch.*

The sight of Dean's name cut sharpest. Patrick squeezed his eyes shut, memory flashing, tears soaking his pillow, muffled sobs rattling his chest. He had faintly registered a knock at his door sometime in the night, soft and persistent, but he'd been too wrecked to move, too hollowed out to answer.

Now the weight of it sat heavily on him, an ache behind his eyes, a sour taste of regret. He set the phone face down, unable to keep looking at it, and dragged himself out of bed. His body moved like stone, every step an act of willpower.

He went through the motions of getting ready—shower, clothes, the whole autopilot ritual of survival. When he caught sight of himself in the mirror, eyes swollen, cheeks blotchy, he winced. RADA awaited, and with it, Dean.

He couldn't walk in broken. He couldn't let them see.

So he did what he'd trained his whole life to do: he performed. He layered on the neutral face, the easy smile, the practiced lift of the brow. He rehearsed his lines in the mirror, not Shakespeare but the Patrick O'Connell version of *I'm fine.*

By the time he stepped into the rehearsal room, he wore the mask like armor.

Dean was already there. His gaze lifted immediately, landing on Patrick across the space. Concern flickered openly in his hazel eyes, heavy and searching, the kind of look that could undo a person if they let it.

Patrick's own gaze snapped away, down to the script in his hands. *Pretend the Bard has all the answers. Pretend it's just the words, not the wreckage inside your chest.*

He could feel Dean's eyes linger on him anyway, like a hand brushing too close to an open wound. The silence between them thrummed beneath the classroom chatter, loud in its own way, a question neither of them dared voice.

Patrick held the mask tighter, even as his insides screamed.

The rehearsal break was a mercy. Patrick slipped into a corner of the studio, gripping his script like it might anchor him. He was working on steadying his breath when Monty appeared, sliding into the chair beside him with that unbothered, too-casual ease that usually meant he'd clocked something.

"Hey, Pat," Monty said quietly, dropping his voice so only Patrick could hear. "I saw what went down last night with Jacob. And I overheard him running his mouth earlier. Now he's been telling people you and Dean are a thing. Trying to stir shit."

Patrick's chest flared hot. *That fucker.*

Monty's expression hardened, rare steel in his voice. "Don't let him get to you. He's trying to look important. He's just an insecure asshole with a sword."

Patrick swallowed, throat tight, but nodded. He couldn't trust his voice not to break.

The true test came a few minutes later when Garrett called them back into the circle. Today's scene: Act I, Scene V. The pilgrim lips moment. The kiss.

Patrick stood at the perimeter with the rest of the ensemble, his stomach curling into knots. He watched as Dean stepped into the center. Opposite him, smirking and adjusting his cuffs, stood Jacob.

It was a nightmare tableau: the boy who had broken

his heart last night acting opposite the boy who thought personal space was just a gap waiting to be filled.

"This is the spark," Garrett said, pacing as his gaze swept between them. "Romeo, you are drawn in, helpless. Julius, you resist but cannot deny the pull. This kiss is the shift. The point of no return. The audience must feel that fire."

Patrick's pulse pounded. He forced himself to watch.

Dean (Romeo):

"If I profane with my unworthiest hand this holy shrine, the gentle sin is this. My lips, two blushing pilgrims, ready stand to smooth that rough touch with a tender kiss."

Jacob (Julius):

"Good pilgrim, you do wrong your hand too much, which mannerly devotion shows in this. For saints have hands that pilgrims' hands do touch, and palm to palm is holy palmers' kiss."

Dean's voice was mechanical, lacking its usual warmth.

Dean (Romeo):

"Have not saints lips, and holy palmers too?"

Jacob (Julius):

"Ay, pilgrim, lips that they must use in prayer."

Jacob stepped closer, invading Dean's space with a leering intensity that felt wrong for the character—too aggressive, too knowing.

Dean (Romeo):

"O, then, dear saint, let lips do what hands do. They pray. Grant thou, lest turn to despair."

Jacob (Julius):

"Saints do not move, though grant for prayers' sake."

The moment hung, breath suspended. Jacob leaned in, lips puckered in a mocking exaggeration, waiting.

Dean hesitated. A flicker of something unreadable passed through his eyes—disgust, exhaustion, conflict. His body stilled.

Then, he pulled back abruptly, stepping out of the scene.

The silence cracked like glass.

Garrett's brow furrowed. "Dean?"

Dean rubbed the back of his neck, not looking at Jacob. "I'm sorry, Garrett. I can't. I don't think I'm ready for that yet. The kiss. It... I'm not in the right headspace."

Jacob let out a sharp, derisive laugh. "Not in the headspace? It's acting, man. Though I suppose you're used to everything being handed to you on a silver platter."

"Jacob," Garrett warned.

But Jacob turned on Dean, stepping close, his voice dropping to a sneer that carried across the silent room. "What's the matter, Clarke? Not your type? Or would you do it if it was Patrick standing here?"

Patrick froze, the blood draining from his face.

Jacob smirked, glancing over at Patrick before locking

eyes with Dean again. "You two seem like you'd enjoy that sort of thing. Bet you've been rehearsing it in private, haven't you?"

Dean's head snapped up. His eyes went dark. "What the fuck did you just say?"

"You heard me," Jacob spat.

Dean stepped forward, chest heaving. But before he could speak, Jacob shoved him hard in the chest.

"Back off, pretty boy!" Jacob yelled.

Dean stumbled back but regained his balance instantly. The restraint snapped. He didn't throw a punch, but he grabbed Jacob by the collar, shoving him back.

Jacob didn't hesitate. He swung, hitting Dean hard in the face.

The room erupted in chaos. Dean stumbled, clutching his jaw, but Jacob lunged again. The two of them grappled, crashing to the floor in a tangle of limbs. Jacob was wild, furious, trying to land a cheap shot while Dean was down, his fist raised.

"Enough!" Garrett's roar shook the walls.

Garrett was there in seconds, hauling Jacob off Dean by the back of his shirt and throwing him backward.

"Get off him!" Garrett bellowed.

Dean scrambled up, chest heaving, a red mark blooming on his cheekbone. Jacob stood panting, straightening his shirt, a wild, defiant look in his eyes.

"You're done," Garrett said, his voice deadly quiet.

Jacob blinked. "What?"

"You're out of the show. You're out of this company," Garrett said, pointing to the door. "Get your things and get out."

Jacob's face twisted into a mask of petulant rage. "You can't do that! I'll tell my parents about this! You'll be fired!"

"Tell them," Garrett said, stepping closer, towering over him. "Tell them you assaulted a castmate in my rehearsal room. Go."

Jacob looked around the room, searching for support, but found only cold stares. He scoffed, grabbed his bag, and stormed out, slamming the heavy door behind him.

The silence in the wake of the slam was deafening.

Garrett exhaled a long breath, adjusting his jacket. He turned to the ensemble, his eyes landing squarely on Patrick.

"Patrick," Garrett said firmly. "You're on."

Patrick blinked, his heart hammering against his ribs. "What?"

"You are Julius," Garrett stated. "Start prepping. We run the scene again in ten minutes."

Garrett turned and marched toward his office, leaving the room reeling.

Patrick stood rooted to the spot. Julius. He was the lead. It was everything he had wanted, everything he had worked for—but it felt wrong in every way.

Dean was still standing in the center of the room,

wiping a spot of blood from his face.

Patrick took a step forward, instinct overriding his anger. "Dean…"

Dean looked up. He saw Patrick and immediately started walking toward him, ignoring the whispers of the other students.

"Patrick," Dean said, his voice breathless, eyes wide and pleading. "Patrick—last night—I…"

He reached out, as if to touch Patrick's arm.

Patrick flinched back.

The movement was small, but it stopped Dean dead in his tracks. The image of the club, the kiss, the betrayal, it all rushed back, colliding with the violence of the last five minutes.

"Not now, Dean," Patrick said, his voice trembling.

"But I need to explain—" Dean started.

"I said not now," Patrick cut him off, his voice cracking.

He walked away, heading toward the corner to grab his script, leaving Dean standing alone in the center of the floor.

The rehearsal room emptied slowly, everyone hushed and unsettled by Jacob's outburst. Patrick lingered at the edge, dread already coiling in his gut. He didn't need to be told Garrett wanted to see him, he could feel it, like gravity pulling him toward the inevitable.

"Patrick," Garrett said, his tone clipped but not

unkind. "My office."

The walk there felt like a death march. Patrick's shoes echoed against the hallway floorboards, each step heavy with the certainty that he'd finally ruined everything. Garrett's office smelled of old paper and dust, the narrow space lined with shelves of scripts and marked-up folios.

"Sit," Garrett said, gesturing to the chair opposite his desk. He remained standing, arms crossed, his dark eyes fixed on Patrick like a surgeon about to cut.

"What's going on?" Garrett's voice was quieter now, even, but no less commanding. "I know that was…a lot. But now you are stepping up. And I need to know where your head is."

Garrett leaned against his desk, crossing his arms. "I watched you just now. You got the role of a lifetime, and you look like you're attending a funeral. Is it what Jacob said?"

Patrick stared at the scuffed floorboards, his throat closing. He wanted to lie. But Garrett's gaze pinned him in place. The dam broke.

"I can't—" Patrick's voice cracked. "I can't pretend it's just the work."

And then it all spilled out.

The birthday. Jacob's drunken advances. Dean's protectiveness. The sharp, unbearable image of Dean kissing Olivia under the strobe lights. The fight just now. Every fear, every wound, every humiliation poured out of him in a rush, raw and unfiltered.

His voice shook. "I'm such an idiot. I let myself feel something again, and of course it's for someone who's not even available. And now I have to play his lover? I can't do this. I can't act opposite him."

"Patrick," Garrett interrupted, firm but not unkind. He leaned forward. "You're not an idiot. You're human. And humans fall. Hard."

Patrick blinked through tears, stunned into silence.

"Dean's hesitation with Jacob… That wasn't just about Jacob," Garrett said softly. "And whatever is happening between you two personally, you have to channel it."

Garrett's voice dropped lower. "Don't let someone else's journey make you doubt your worth. Or your truth. You've been brave enough to open your heart. Now be brave enough to stand in that truth, no matter how messy it feels."

The words landed like stones in water, rippling through him. Patrick wiped at his eyes.

Garrett didn't press further. He simply said, "Go rest. We'll work again tomorrow."

Patrick nodded, too drained to speak, and stumbled back out into the corridor.

By the time he reached Schaffer House, exhaustion pressed heavy on his shoulders. He collapsed onto his narrow bed. His phone lay on the desk, face-up. Missed calls from Dean. Missed calls from Jess.

Now, in the quiet, he needed a voice. The one that had always cut through the noise. His mom.

Patrick's thumb hovered, then pressed call.

"Hi, my love," she answered after a few rings. "You sound worn out. What's going on?"

Patrick swallowed hard. "I got the lead, Mom."

"Patrick! That's amazing!"

"It doesn't feel amazing," he whispered. "Do you remember the guy Dean I told you about?"

"Yes, I remember. What about him?"

His throat tightened. "I think I'm falling for him. And it terrifies me. One moment it feels like he's right there, and the next he pulls away. And then last night I saw him kiss a girl in our group. And now I have to act in love with him every day."

"Oh, honey," his mother murmured. "You can't keep that inside. If you care for him, you need to be honest."

Patrick's voice cracked. "But what if I'm just part of him figuring things out? What if I'm just a phase?"

"Then at least you'll know," she said. "And if he's uncertain, that has more to do with his journey than with you."

Patrick shut his eyes, tears slipping free. "What if he chooses Olivia?"

Her voice softened. "Then it will hurt, yes. But it won't change who you are. You are worthy of someone who sees you completely. Don't ever forget that."

He pressed a fist to his mouth, trying to breathe through the aches and tears.

"And remember you are there," she added gently. "The stage has always been your anchor. It's where you turn your feelings into something true. Don't lose that now."

Patrick exhaled shakily. "Thanks, Mom."

"I love you," she said softly.

"I love you too."

When the call ended, Patrick sat in silence, Garrett's words and his mother's weaving together like fragile threads. He still felt raw but not empty. Not entirely lost.

CHAPTER 14

I t was later that evening when the RADA groups made their way to the Bridge Theatre for *A Midsummer Night's Dream.*

Even though Patrick felt like a human-shaped bruise—emotionally drained, sleep-deprived, and reeling from the sudden, terrifying weight of the casting change—he knew he had to go. He told himself it was for professional reasons: exposure to new interpretations, critical observation, the noble pursuit of "learning through art."

But the truth was simpler and much less noble. He wanted a moment with Dean. Just one. Something normal, grounding, a chance to reset after the emotional demolition he just endured.

The theater itself was sleek and modern. Its minimalist geometry stood in stark contrast to the lush, glittering chaos of the world they were about to enter. The rest of their group buzzed with energy, half talking about the play, half whispering about Jacob's spectacular exit and Garrett's fury.

Dean was already in the row ahead, laughing at something Jess said. In the harsh lobby lights, Patrick could see the faint swelling on Dean's cheekbone where Jacob had hit him. That sound—bright, familiar, determinedly unbothered—both steadied and gutted him.

The house lights dimmed. Darkness folded over the crowd. A low hum of anticipation filled the air, the collective inhale of hundreds of people waiting for a story to begin.

And then, just like that, magic.

The production was chaotic and clever, bursting with color and life.

Patrick found himself laughing, not the polite, theater laugh he'd perfected but something real. For two blessed acts, he forgot heartbreak, forgot the script burning a hole in his bag, and forgot the text messages left unread.

He remembered why he loved this world.

Every so often, in the flicker of stage lights, Patrick caught Dean's profile, rapt, unguarded, his expression open and soft. That was the danger of Dean: He could make the world feel illuminated and safe in the same breath that he broke your heart.

During intermission, they drifted together in a knot of classmates near the bar, drinks in hand, laughter spilling too easily. Jess was halfway through a rant about Oberon's leather jacket when Dean turned to Patrick.

"Feeling any better?" Dean asked.

"Define good." Patrick gave a half-smile.

"Better than yesterday then," Dean's mouth quirked.

"That's a low bar." Patrick rolled his eyes.

"Then you're clearing it," Dean said, warmth tucked just under the tease.

Patrick rolled his eyes, but the corner of his mouth betrayed him. Something small and tentative began to thaw between them, not forgiveness, exactly, but the possibility of it.

When the lights dimmed again, he felt a strange, fragile lightness. Lovers chased each other through neon forests, the world blurred with enchantment, and Patrick thought, *Maybe this is what healing feels like. Not one grand moment of clarity but a series of small, stubborn choices to keep showing up.*

He wasn't ready to give up yet.

When the show ended, the crowd spilled out in a warm, humming tide of laughter and chatter. The air outside was cool and smelled faintly of rain and popcorn, the kind of London night that shimmered with life. The lights of Tower Bridge glowed along the river, reflected gold and unsteady on the water.

Patrick lingered near the exit, half-listening as Jess debated the ending with Monty, her hands slicing the air in animated gestures. Dean stood a few feet away, head tilted back as he laughed at something Olivia said, and that sound, bright, familiar, effortlessly warm, was enough to undo every bit of composure Patrick had managed to rebuild.

He couldn't do another night of pretending. Not after everything. He needed air. He needed clarity.

"Dean," Patrick said, touching his elbow gently, "could we talk for a minute?"

"Now?" Dean asked, his brows lifting.

"Yeah," Patrick said, steadying his voice, "just a walk. Two minutes."

Their classmates continued down the steps toward the restaurants, voices rising in cheerful chaos. Dean hesitated, then nodded once. "Alright," he said softly, "let's walk."

They peeled off from the group and followed the path that curved along the Thames. The city hummed quietly around them, the low rush of cars, the faint echo of laughter, the shuffle of footsteps on wet pavement.

They stopped at the railing overlooking the water. Tower Bridge stretched ahead, its reflection broken by the slow pulse of the tide. Patrick gripped the cold metal, grounding himself against the urge to flee. He could feel Dean's warmth beside him, close but not touching.

"I need to be honest with you," Patrick said, surprised by how even his voice sounded, "about everything."

"Okay," Dean said, resting his hands beside Patrick's on the railing, "I'm listening."

"This summer's been…perfect," Patrick said, exhaling shakily. "Not because of RADA or London—though those have been incredible—but because of you. You've made me laugh when I thought I couldn't. You've made me feel seen in ways I didn't think I deserved. Being around you has felt like finding sunlight again."

He turned toward him fully, heart pounding. "You're extraordinary, Dean," he said. "The way you care about people, the way you hide it like it's something to be embarrassed about. The way you see the world, like it's fragile and worth protecting. You make me want to be braver—not just on stage, but here, now, with you. And it doesn't hurt that you're one of the most beautiful fucking people I've ever met," Patrick added, a shaky laugh breaking through. "Honestly, it's rude. Distracting, really."

Dean laughed, the sound breaking the tension like sunlight through storm clouds.

"You're ridiculous," he said, ducking his head.

"Probably," Patrick said, smiling, "but it's still true."

Patrick reached up to his neck. He felt the cool silver chain against his skin, the weight of the compass against his collarbone, the one he had put on just last night in a moment of defiance.

He unclasped it.

He held the necklace between them, the silver compass catching the bridge lights.

"There are two of them," Patrick said softly. "I have the matching one back at the dorm."

Dean looked at the necklace, then back at Patrick,

listening intently.

"When I bought them in New York, I thought I knew who they were for," he said. "I didn't. This one... it was always meant for you."

He placed it gently in Dean's palm, his thumb brushing over the metal. "Even if nothing else comes of this, even if you decide you don't feel the same, I want you to have it," he said. "Because it's something that connects us. A reminder of what this summer was. You've already changed my life more than you know."

He closed Dean's hand around it and said, "That's all. That's the truth."

"Patrick..." Dean began, looking down at the pendant, his thumb tracing the edge. His expression shifted—confusion, emotion, something Patrick couldn't name.

Patrick looked down at the dark water, blinking back the hot sting of tears. "God, Dean, I won't lie. It will destroy me. But this silence? Pretending I'm just your friend while my chest aches every time you walk into a room? That's worse. It's eating me alive."

He looked up, his eyes wet and searching, desperate for Dean to understand.

"Especially now," Patrick whispered, his breath hitching. "I can't look at you on stage and lie about what I feel."

A breeze came off the river, cool and insistent, lifting their hair and turning the golden reflection of the bridge into rippling light.

"I hear you," Dean said, stepping closer, his voice low.

"Okay," Patrick said, his throat tightening so much it hurt.

"I saw you," Dean said quietly. "The way you looked at me on your birthday…and then today, when I tried to reach for you after the fight, and you flinched. I know I hurt you. And I'm not going to make excuses. I just…I know."

Patrick nodded, the acknowledgment landing like a fragile mercy, something real and human.

"I haven't done this before," Dean said, turning the compass over once before slipping it into his pocket. "Not like this. I'm trying to understand what's real, what's me, and what's fear. I don't want to say the wrong thing because I'm too afraid to say the right one."

"I don't need perfect," Patrick said softly. "Just honesty."

They stood in the quiet hum of the city, the river whispering below. Somewhere behind them, laughter drifted through the night. The air between them was thick, charged with everything unsaid.

"Dean, I think…" Patrick breathed, a tear finally escaping, tracking hot down his cheek.

"I think I'm falling—"

"There you two are," Jess's voice called out from down the path, completely oblivious to the moment she was interrupting.

Jess's voice cut through the moment like a bright ribbon, Monty right beside her, both of them grinning as if they'd just burst out of another play. "We're starving. You're coming, yeah? Dean, your turn to buy. Price of fame," she said, looping an arm loosely toward them.

Monty gave a low whistle, eyes flicking between them with barely contained mischief. "You two look like you've been plotting state secrets," he said. "Come on before the line's impossible."

Patrick blinked, reality crashing back like cold water. He tried to shape his face into something casual, something that didn't scream *I was about to emotionally combust by the Thames.*

Dean's hand rose as if to steady him, fingers brushing Patrick's arm before settling lightly at his shoulder. "We'll catch up," he said to the group, his voice steady but quiet. "One minute."

"Make it thirty seconds," Jess said, already moving toward the street. "The line for chips is apocalyptic."

Laughter trailed after them, dissolving into the night. When they were alone again, the moment still hovered, bruised, delicate, alive. The hum of the river filled the space where words might have been.

"I have to gather my thoughts," Dean said, still close enough that Patrick could feel the warmth of his breath. "I want to tell you something. But not yet. I need a moment to process this. To understand it in a way that's fair to you. Give me until tomorrow."

"Tomorrow," Patrick repeated, the word landing in his chest like a stone and a promise at once. "Okay."

"Thank you," Dean said softly, and the gratitude in his tone made Patrick's heart ache in a different way, quieter, deeper.

They turned toward the street again, walking side by side. The air had cooled, the wind off the water sharper now, but the lights still shimmered gold across the river.

At the edge of the crowd, Jess threw her arm in the air like a conductor summoning an orchestra. "Come on, the world's saddest salad awaits," she called, grinning.

Dean's hand slipped from Patrick's shoulder to the middle of his back, a touch so small it could've been nothing, but to Patrick it felt like everything.

"Let's go," Dean said quietly, his voice low enough that only Patrick heard.

They stepped forward together, into the noise and movement and ordinary chaos of post-show London. Jess was already talking about the fairy costumes; Monty was complaining about overpriced chips; someone was singing something off key in the distance. The city thrummed around them, alive and relentless.

Patrick let the sound wash over him. His pulse was still uneven, but lighter now. He didn't know which way tomorrow would tilt, whether Dean's words would bring clarity or another kind of heartbreak. But he knew this: He had said what he needed to say, and Dean had asked for time.

It wasn't certainty, but it wasn't silence either.

The night stretched open ahead of them, full of neon and salt and laughter. Patrick followed, the river at his side, the bridge gleaming above, the compass hidden safely in Dean's pocket, and hope, thin but real, moving with him like breath.

CHAPTER 15

Patrick woke the next day to a familiar knot of anxiety in his stomach, but beneath it, a fragile thread of hope, almost a delicate silver filament.

Dean's words from the night before, *"I want to tell you something. But not yet. I need a moment to process this. To understand it in a way that's fair to you,"* replayed in his mind, a tantalizing, agonizing riddle he couldn't stop dissecting.

Every syllable echoed, every pause felt loaded with unspoken meaning. He checked his phone almost compulsively, every few minutes, as if the sheer force of his anticipation could conjure a message, willing it to light up with Dean's name.

The morning classes were a blur. Patrick moved through them like a ghost, his body present, but his mind miles away. He was carrying the physical weight of his new reality in his bag: the Julius script, covered in Jacob's aggressive scribbles, which Patrick had stayed up half the night trying to memorize.

He tried to focus on his voice exercises, on the intricate movements of their dance class, but every instruction from Diana felt muffled, every step heavy. He stole glances at Dean across the room, trying to decipher his expression.

Dean seemed quieter than usual, his brow furrowed in thought, occasionally running a hand through his perpetually disheveled hair. He looked as though he was wrestling with something profound, something that consumed his every thought, mirroring Patrick's own internal turmoil. This shared, unspoken tension was a constant, almost physical presence between them.

During their *Romeo and Julius* rehearsals, the tension was almost unbearable. It wasn't just the romantic tension anymore; it was the professional terror.

Patrick stood center stage, clutching the script like a life raft because he hadn't had weeks to learn the blocking like everyone else.

He found himself constantly distracted, his gaze drifting towards Dean, who was running lines with Olivia on the side. He felt a frantic impatience, a desperate need for clarity. The words of Shakespeare, usually a comforting anchor, now felt like a cruel mockery.

He botched lines, missed cues, and tripped over his own feet trying to read and walk at the same time. Garrett's usually sharp critiques felt like distant echoes, unable to penetrate the thick fog of his anxiety.

"Patrick, focus!" Garrett's voice boomed, startling him

from his reverie. "Your Julius is distracted. I know you are catching up, but you must be present! Where is his mind?"

"I…sorry," Patrick mumbled, cheeks flushing as he tried to re-center himself, but it was futile. His mind was a relentless loop of *what ifs* and *what nows*. Was Dean regretting their conversation, his words, everything? The thought was a cold, sharp knife twisting in his gut.

Lunch was a silent affair. Patrick sat with Jess, picking at his food, unable to swallow. Jess, ever perceptive, gave him a sympathetic look.

"Still no word?" she whispered, her voice gentle.

"Nothing. Just…'a moment.' It's killing me, Jess," Patrick said, shaking his head, a silent, miserable confession.

"He'll come around, Pat," Jess said, squeezing his hand. "He's probably just processing. It's a big thing, what you told him. Give him time. And remember, you were incredibly brave. No matter what happens."

Her words were a small comfort, a tiny flicker of warmth in the cold grip of his anxiety.

The afternoon dragged on, each minute an eternity. Patrick watched the clock, willing the hands to move faster.

Finally, just as the last class of the day ended, a notification popped up. It was Dean. Patrick's heart leaped into his throat, doing a nervous somersault.

He snatched his phone, his fingers trembling.

Dean: *Meet me at Waterloo Bridge at 7:30 PM. Sunset.*

A wave of nerves washed over Patrick, so potent it almost made him sway. This was it. The conversation they hadn't finished. The answer he desperately needed.

Patrick left RADA with his pulse already loud in his ears. The city felt sharpened at the edges, as if someone had turned up the contrast. He cut through the fading evening crowds, past office workers loosening ties, tourists holding paper maps that folded and unfolded like wings, couples walking shoulder to shoulder in easy silence.

He tried to regulate his breathing the way Diana had drilled them in class. *"In for four, hold for four, out for six."* It helped for a few steps, then his mind sprinted ahead again, chasing the shape of the conversation he had been waiting for all day.

The sky was a slow-breathing canvas, pale gold washing into rose, then deeper mauves far to the east. Low clouds carried the last color like bruised petals. A cyclist chimed a bell and slipped past. Someone laughed behind him, and the sound was so bright he almost flinched.

On the South Bank, the river path was alive. A child let go of a balloon and cried as it climbed without mercy. A vendor folded up postcards, the cardboard edges rasping against one another. Patrick took it all in, and none of it stuck. His thoughts kept pinwheeling back to the message glowing on his phone.

He checked the time again. Too early, then suddenly not early enough. He walked more slowly, then sped up without meaning to. He ran a hand through his hair, and it refused to settle.

As Waterloo Bridge grew near, the river widened in his vision, a dark strip of moving glass lit with scattered coins of light. The first stars shouldered their way into the sky. A breeze came up off the water and crept under the collar of his sweater. He shivered and kept walking.

He told himself not to script it. He had done enough of that already. He told himself to be present, to listen, to accept whatever came.

Music drifted in before he saw the guitarist. The melody tugged at him like a hand. *The Kinks. 'Waterloo Sunset.'* His throat tightened. He fished in his pocket for coins and let them clatter into the open case, the metal sound bright in the evening. The guitarist gave a nod without looking up.

Patrick turned and searched the bridge.

Dean was coming from the far side, moving in and out of the traffic of bodies. The last of the light caught in his hair. He held a single red rose by the stem, not hiding it, not flaunting it, simply carrying it. The compass necklace lay against his chest, catching and releasing the glow as he walked toward Patrick. For a heartbeat, Patrick could not feel his feet.

"Did you tell him to play that?" Patrick asked because he had to say something or he would come apart. His voice betrayed him only a little.

"Maybe," Dean said, his mouth curving slightly.

The small answer loosened something in Patrick's chest. He nodded and looked at Dean's face, really looked. He saw nerves in the tightness around Dean's eyes, the controlled steadiness of his breath, the decision sitting just behind all of it.

Dean stepped closer, not touching. The rose turned slowly between his fingers.

"Patrick." He paused, then tried again. "Patrick, I'm sorry. About Olivia. It was nothing. It was stupid, and I was drunk. She's a friend. That's all."

He glanced down at the compass, his thumb brushing its edge, then lifted his gaze and held Patrick's.

"And rehearsal. And last night, when you told me everything. I didn't know how to respond. Not because I didn't feel anything. Because I did. I do."

His voice caught. He swallowed and tried again, words uneven but honest.

"I've never been with a guy before. Not once. I didn't have the language for what I've been feeling. With Chloe, everything was easy. Comfortable. Expected. It was a path I could walk with my eyes half-closed. And when something else flickered at the edges, I pushed it down. I told myself it didn't matter. That it would pass if I didn't stare at it."

Dean took a shaky breath, his gaze dropping to the river below.

"But it's more than that," Dean said. "You know about my sister. You know what happened."

Patrick nodded silently.

"Since she died," Dean continued, his knuckles white around the stem of the rose, "I've felt this crushing pressure to be…enough. To be the perfect son. My parents are broken, Patrick. They hang on by a thread. And I've spent years terrifying myself that if I step one foot out of line, if I cause a scandal, or confusion, or anything 'abnormal,' it'll be the thing that finally breaks them."

Dean looked up, eyes glistening.

"Being with a man? That wasn't in the plan. It's complicated. It's not the safe, traditional life they probably picture for me. And I was so scared that if I let myself feel this, I'd be letting them down."

Patrick's heart ached, a physical pang in his chest. He took a half-step forward, wanting to reach out, but letting Dean finish.

"Then I met you. From the first class we had together, you got under my skin. The way you listen. You make me want to be better. You make the room feel different when you're in it. The stupid jokes that made me laugh when I was trying not to. Regent's Park, you were next to me, and your head tipped onto my shoulder, and I didn't move because it felt like the most natural thing in the world."

He rubbed his knuckles over his mouth, still searching.

"When I kissed Olivia, I think I was trying to prove

something to myself. That I was fine. That this was nothing. It felt like watching myself from outside, doing the sensible thing. It wasn't fair to her, and it wasn't fair to you. I'm sorry."

Silence pressed in for a heartbeat, filled only by guitar and river and the faraway hiss of buses.

"Last night, when you handed me the necklace," Dean said, his voice softer now, "it felt like you put a mirror in front of me. A choice. I went home, and I couldn't stop holding it. I kept thinking about the way you said you had one too. That even if I couldn't…even if I couldn't step into this, you wanted something that could still connect us. Who does that? Who's that generous when they're afraid? You are."

He let out a breath that shivered at the edges. "I panicked," Dean admitted, a wry, self-deprecating laugh escaping him. "I didn't trust myself to make the jump alone. So…I met with Jess this morning."

Patrick blinked, surprised. "Jess?"

Dean nodded. "I confessed everything to her. How I felt about you. How terrified I was of my parents, of the pressure, of not knowing how to be with a man. I asked her not to say anything to you because I needed to be the one to do this. But she…she told me how much you care. She made me realize that hiding to keep my parents comfortable was just making me miserable."

He stepped the smallest fraction closer. The rose bent

between his fingers.

"I've been falling for you," he said. "Not in a tidy, cinematic way. In a messy, interrupting-my-sleep kind of way. In the way that I'm halfway through a line, and I think of you, and I lose my place. In the way where the idea of you not being in my day makes everything look gray.

"I look at you, Patrick, and I don't just see a friend," Dean whispered. "I see the person who reminds me how to be alive. And that terrifies me, because I finally have something I can't bear to lose. But God, I would rather risk my heart with you every single day than keep it safe and empty without you."

Patrick let out a strangled sound, a sob catching in his throat.

He saw it then, the sheer magnitude of what Dean was offering. It wasn't just a crush. Dean was handing him his grief, his fear, and his hope, all wrapped up in shaking hands.

Patrick moved closer, his own eyes blurring with tears.

"You're not alone in this," Patrick said, his hands coming up to cup Dean's face, his thumbs brushing away the tears that were finally spilling onto Dean's cheeks. "Do you hear me? You don't have to carry that pressure anymore. Not with me."

Dean let out a shuddering breath, leaning his forehead against Patrick's, his body finally sagging as the weight he'd been carrying began to slip.

"I've got you," Patrick whispered fiercely, tears tracking down his own face now, mingling with Dean's where their skin touched. "We'll figure it out. Your parents, the world, everything. But right here? You're safe."

"I want you," Dean breathed, his voice wet and raw.

"I'm right here," Patrick promised.

Dean's eyes shone in the fading light, and then he moved, closing the sliver of distance between them. His gaze flicked down to Patrick's lips, lingering.

The kiss was soft at first, tentative, the brush of lips testing the shape of possibility. Patrick felt the world tilt. His hands tightened slightly on Dean's face, grounding himself in the reality of the moment. Dean responded, deepening the kiss with a slow, aching hunger, as if every unspoken word, every sleepless night, every suppressed longing was pouring into this one act.

The city melted away. The music, the river, the passing footsteps, all of it blurred into a hum at the edge of consciousness. There was only Dean's mouth against his, warm and sure and trembling, and the taste of mint, and the small, desperate sound Dean made when Patrick kissed him back harder.

Patrick's arms slid down to wrap around Dean's waist, pulling him close. He felt the steady beat of Dean's heart against his own racing chest. Dean's hands threaded into his hair, holding him there, as if afraid Patrick might vanish if he let go. They kissed until breathing was no longer optional, until they pulled back just far enough to press their foreheads together, gasping, laughing softly in disbelief.

Patrick's lips tingled. His whole body hummed like it had been rewired.

"That," Dean said hoarsely, his voice thick with wonder, "was our first real kiss. And it was perfect."

Patrick laughed, breathless, tears stinging his eyes. "Better than perfect."

Dean wiped at the corner of his eye with his thumb, smiling in that unguarded way that always undid Patrick. "I didn't want it to happen in rehearsal. I didn't want it to be a performance. I needed it to be this. Just us. Just now."

Patrick kissed him again, softer this time, a tender punctuation to Dean's words. "It was," he murmured against his lips. "Ours."

They stood like that, wrapped around each other, as the last blush of sunset gave way to twilight. The compass necklace glinted faintly between them, a small, steady star against Dean's chest. The rose, somehow still intact, was caught between their joined hands.

"So you *did* tell the guitarist to play 'Waterloo Sunset,' didn't you?" Patrick asked, his voice wobbling with a laugh that was half-sob.

"I thought it was appropriate," Dean said, his grin breaking wide, sheepish and delighted all at once. "Felt right. Like a soundtrack for tonight."

Patrick let out a disbelieving laugh, pressing his face briefly into Dean's shoulder. "You're ridiculous."

"And you love it," Dean said, his tone half-joking, half-pleading.

"I do," Patrick said, meeting his gaze. "God help me, I do."

They kissed again, longer this time, until Patrick felt dizzy with it, until he knew with bone-deep certainty that everything had shifted, that nothing would ever be the same.

When they finally broke apart, the world eased back into focus: the glow of streetlamps on the bridge, the guitarist sliding into another verse, the murmur of the Thames beneath them. But Patrick felt untouchable, as though he were standing in a circle of light that nothing could breach.

"I don't know what comes next," Dean admitted quietly, brushing his knuckles over Patrick's cheek, tender and reverent. "But I want to find out. With you."

"Then we'll find out together," Patrick said, his chest aching with joy.

For a while, they just stood in each other's arms, listening to the song, breathing in time, two figures silhouetted against the fading light of London.

CHAPTER 16

The next few days were less of a schedule and more of a hostile takeover of Patrick's central nervous system, sponsored by caffeine strong enough to restart a heart that stopped three days ago, and the distinct, vibrating terror that he might walk on stage and forget the English language entirely.

If anyone thought stepping into the lead role with forty-eight hours' notice was a dream come true, they've clearly never had that dream where you show up to school naked and unprepared. This was exactly that, only with more velvet and a very sharp sword.

Jacob had possessed weeks to learn the blocking, the lines, and the complex sword-fighting choreography. Patrick had, by his estimation, about twelve minutes.

He attacked the role with a ferocity that bordered on unhinged. He was the first one in the studio in the morning, muttering lines to the empty walls. He spent hours erasing Jacob's script notes, which turned out to be less about character motivation and more just reminders to "smolder harder" next to doodles of his own abs.

And yet...the rehearsals transformed.

With the secret of their feelings finally out in the open, acknowledged and sealed by the Thames, the air between Patrick and Dean shifted. The jagged, unspoken tension that had plagued them since the birthday night evaporated, replaced by a current of trust that hummed beneath every line.

Also, Dean kept looking at him. Like, *really* looking at him. It was distracting. It was excellent. It was a serious workplace hazard.

Garrett stopped them halfway through the balcony scene on Thursday afternoon. He stood with his arms folded, a silence stretching out that usually meant someone was about to get emotionally shredded in front of their peers.

Patrick braced himself. *Here we go,* he thought. *Tell me I possess the romantic charisma of a damp sponge. Tell me I'm ruining the legacy of the Bard.*

Instead, a slow, cat-that-got-the-cream smile spread across Garrett's face.

"Yes. That. Exactly that," Garrett said with relish. "Patrick, you aren't just reciting the poetry anymore; you are wielding it. And Dean... you're finally listening to him."

Dean's half-smile slid in, his arm fitting around Patrick's waist as if it belonged there. Patrick's brain short-circuited briefly. He forgot his own middle name. "We're working on it."

"Excellent." Garrett's grin widened. "Bottle it. Infuse every word and look with that honesty. The audience will feel it before they know it."

Patrick walked off stage looking around for the hidden camera crew. Surely this was a prank.

They broke for lunch on a high. Patrick grabbed his tray and slid into the seat across from Jess, who was currently dissecting a tangerine with the surgical precision of a serial killer.

"You look like you just won the lottery," Jess noted. "Or Garrett actually complimented you, which is statistically rarer. Like seeing a unicorn. Or a straight man in a musical theater program."

"Both," Patrick admitted. "It's...it's clicking, Jess. The scenes. I feel like I finally own the role."

Jess smiled, softer than usual. "You were never just filling in, Pat. You're the lead. You earned it."

Patrick looked down at his hands, then back up at her. "Hey. I need to say something. And don't make a face, I'm trying to be sincere."

Jess raised an eyebrow. "Oh god. Is this the emotional part?"

"Shut up and listen." Patrick laughed, though his chest felt tight. "Dean told me. About the morning after the fight. That he came to you."

Jess paused, her expression shifting from teasing to sincere. "Yeah. He was a mess, Pat. A terrified, beautiful mess."

"He told me you were the one who got through to him. That you reassured him." Patrick reached across the table, covering her hand with his. "Thank you, Jess. Seriously. I don't know if he would have met me on that bridge if you hadn't talked him off the ledge."

Jess squeezed his hand back, her eyes shining. "I didn't do anything he wasn't already feeling. I just gave him a little shove. But...I am really proud of you. Both of you. Watching you two figure this out, while dealing with the show and the pressure? It's been... well, it's been a lot. But you're doing it."

"We are," Patrick said, a quiet sense of accomplishment settling over him.

From then on, the production gathered speed. By Friday night, they were exhausted. They had run the tomb scene three times. Patrick's knees were bruised from hitting the stage floor, and his voice sounded like he'd been smoking two packs a day since birth.

"Alright, clear the stage!" the stage manager shouted. "That's a wrap for tonight. Go home, sleep, don't speak."

Dean caught Patrick's eye across the wings. He looked as wrecked as Patrick felt—hair messy, shirt untucked, dark circles under his eyes. Patrick wanted to climb him like a tree.

"Drink?"

Patrick smiled tiredly. "God, yes. Gigs?"

Gigs, with its low ceilings, battered tables, and hum of conversation, was their small haven. They slid into their usual window table, thighs brushing as if that had always been the configuration. Two pints arrived, foam high, and they let the noise fold around them like a familiar blanket.

They talked the way they always did here: a loose braid of jokes about fight calls gone wrong, Garrett's dramatic sighs, Jess's commentary, and the odd line-reading that still felt slippery. Beneath it ran something steadier. Dean's knee touched Patrick's and stayed. Fingers lingered too long passing a glass. That unspoken shift glowed, warm and sure.

"Do you ever think how insane this summer's been?" Patrick asked, turning his glass between his hands.

"Every day," Dean said, soft.

Patrick reached for his hand under the table. Their fingers threaded together as if rehearsed. "Feels like a dream I wouldn't dare have. And yet, here we are."

Dean's thumb traced slow circles over his knuckles. "It's real," he murmured. "More real than anything I've felt. You changed everything, Patrick. And watching you work these past few days? Watching you take command of that stage from nothing? It's...it's incredible. I mean it. You're terrifyingly good."

The weight of it pressed tight and sweet against

Patrick's ribs. He broke it with a breathless laugh. "Half the time onstage it's not Julius looking at Romeo. It's me looking at you thinking, how the fuck did I get this lucky?"

Dean flushed, laughing. "You're ridiculous."

"And you love it."

"I do," Dean said, close to his ear, and the words lit Patrick from the inside.

They drained their pints. Splitting up for separate rooms felt suddenly impossible.

"My room's close," Patrick said, pulse wild but steadying under Dean's gaze. "We could go back there."

"I'd like that," Dean said.

Outside, the night air was cool, carrying the faint tang of rain on stone. London thrummed with buses groaning, distant sirens, and voices spilling from doorways. Patrick barely registered any of it. He felt Dean's hand, warm and sure in his, their steps syncing as if they'd always been meant to.

They passed shuttering shopfronts and late cafés still pooling light onto the pavement. A tourist sang a broken line of Oasis off-key. Dean's thumb moved absently across Patrick's knuckles, and that small, unthinking gesture nearly undid him.

They didn't rush, but the current between them pulled tauter with each block. By the time Schaffer House rose ahead, anticipation had sharpened the air to a fine, bright point.

At the entrance, they paused and looked at each other in the lobby's glow.

"Come up?" Patrick asked, voice quiet and steady.

"Yeah," Dean said, with a certainty that eased something deep in Patrick's chest.

The stairwell creaked under their weight, the hush of the building wrapping them like a secret. Patrick unlocked his door. The click of it closing behind them felt like a boundary crossed, the room suddenly charged, humming.

They stood for one suspended beat, just looking, both smiling, both a little shaking with the size of it.

Dean inhaled sharply, his gaze sweeping over Patrick's face as he crossed the distance between them. He cupped Patrick's cheeks, his thumbs gently tracing the contours of his skin. "Patrick..." he murmured.

"I want you," he said, voice low and certain. "All of you."

"God, Dean, I want you too."

He kissed him.

The kiss burned into something unstoppable. It wasn't frantic so much as inevitable, like water breaking through a dam. Dean's mouth moved against his with hunger and reverence both, every brush of lips a vow, every deeper kiss a surrender.

Patrick clung to him, his fingers digging into Dean's back, tracing the curve of muscle like he was trying to memorize it. Dean pressed him against the mattress, his weight grounding, his body hot and solid and real.

They tugged at shirts, fumbling and laughing when Patrick's sleeve got caught, then gasping when bare skin finally met bare skin. Patrick's hands roamed greedily, cataloging each new sensation, the warmth of Dean's shoulders, the sharp line of his collarbone, the dusting of hair on his chest. Dean trembled under his touch, his breath stuttering, as if he couldn't quite believe it was happening either.

It was the release of a week spent holding his breath. All the terror of the role, the pressure of the script, the sheer, unadulterated panic of stepping into the light—it all poured into this. It was a desperate, physical need to feel something other than anxiety. To be grounded. To be real.

"Christ, Patrick," Dean whispered, breaking the kiss only long enough to suck in air. His forehead pressed to Patrick's, their breaths mingling. "You're driving me mad. Do you know that?"

"Am I? And what are you going to do about it?" Patrick's laugh came out shaky, half a sob. He realized he was flirting. He was actually flirting. Somewhere, a choir of angels choked on their harps.

He kissed him again, fiercely, desperately, every ounce of longing poured into the press of his mouth. Dean answered with a groan, low and wrecked, his hands skimming down Patrick's sides, anchoring him, holding him like he was precious.

They tumbled to the bed in a tangle, breathless and grinning between kisses. Dean hovered above him, pausing for a heartbeat, his eyes wide, pupils blown. He searched Patrick's face as though for permission, for certainty.

Patrick lifted a hand, cupping his jaw, his thumb sweeping gently across Dean's lips. "I want this," he said softly, steadily, despite the thunder of his heart. "I want you. All of you."

Dean's throat worked, his voice breaking. "God, I want you too. You have no idea."

They kissed again, slower now, savoring. Dean's mouth trailed down Patrick's neck, finding the sensitive hollow that made Patrick gasp, his body arching instinctively. Dean smiled against his skin, the curve of his lips a teasing question.

Patrick tangled his fingers in Dean's hair, tugging him closer, breath hitching when teeth grazed over his pulse point. "Fuck, Dean."

Dean pulled back just long enough to look at him, his expression tender and almost shy, like a man standing on holy ground. "You're one of the most beautiful fucking people I've ever seen," he said, voice low and raw. "It's annoying."

Patrick burst out laughing, the sound tangled with a moan when Dean kissed him again. The laugh only seemed to undo Dean further, and soon they were both grinning like idiots between kisses, the kind of laughter that came when joy and relief were too big for silence.

Clothes disappeared piece by piece, careless piles on the floor. Each new stretch of skin revealed drew a reverent touch, a whispered curse, a startled gasp. They couldn't seem to stop exploring, hands tracing, mouths discovering, every inch of the other becoming sacred territory.

When Dean finally pressed into him, Patrick gasped, clutching tight, overwhelmed by the sheer intimacy of it, the way Dean whispered his name like a prayer, like a promise. It wasn't hurried. It was careful, almost worshipful, a rhythm that built slowly, every movement an unspoken I'm here, I'm with you.

Patrick wrapped around him, their bodies moving together in perfect, uncoordinated sync, a messy kind of grace. Dean's murmurs spilled against his skin, soft curses, half-formed confessions, Patrick's name over and over until it blurred into music.

It felt endless, and yet Patrick wanted it never to end. He wanted to live inside this moment forever, wrapped in heat and laughter and the raw, terrifying beauty of being known so completely.

When release finally came, it was like a wave breaking, stealing the air from his lungs, leaving him trembling and clinging to Dean. Dean's own cry followed, muffled against Patrick's shoulder, his whole body shuddering as he pressed impossibly closer.

They collapsed together, chests heaving, sheets tangled around their legs, sweat cooling against overheated skin. For a long while, neither spoke. Patrick lay with his head on Dean's chest, listening to the thunder of his heart, grounding himself in its steady rhythm.

Patrick looked up and saw a single tear caught in Dean's lashes, catching the faint light from the window like a diamond.

"God, Patrick. You're so beautiful," Dean whispered.

Patrick's heart hammered against his ribs, not from adrenaline this time, but from the sheer weight of being seen. He reached up, his thumb gently brushing the tear from Dean's cheek.

"Dean," Patrick whispered back. "I'm the luckiest man in the world."

But even as he said it, the reality of it caught in his throat. The timeline. The end of the course. The plane ticket.

Dean pulled back slightly, his brows knitting together as he scanned Patrick's face. "Hey. What is it?"

Patrick swallowed hard, the truth sitting heavy on his tongue. "I'm scared," he admitted. "I'm scared that this... That we end when the summer is over."

Dean let out a shaky breath, a soft, reassuring smile breaking through. He leaned down, pressing his forehead against Patrick's.

"Then I guess I'd better stay right here," Dean

murmured, brushing a soft kiss against Patrick's lips. "Because a summer isn't enough. Let's rewrite the ending."

Patrick surged up, capturing Dean's lips in a kiss that tasted like a promise. When they finally broke apart, breathless and dizzy, Patrick settled back down, curling into the warmth of him.

He rested his head on Dean's chest, listening to the steady, sure rhythm of his heart.

"Good," Patrick whispered into the skin of his chest. "I'd like that."

The last thing Patrick felt before sleep claimed him was Dean's arm pulling him closer, holding him like he was the only solid thing in the world. And for once, Patrick's brain was entirely, blissfully quiet.

CHAPTER 17

The air backstage on opening night was thick with a palpable mix of nerves and exhilarating anticipation. Fear, adrenaline, and the faint nostalgic scent of old theater clung to the velvet curtains, to the greasepaint and hairspray, to every breath drawn in the wings. Twenty-five actors shifted and paced like caged tigers, muttering lines under their breath, flexing hands, adjusting masks and swords. The muffled roar of the audience just beyond was its own heartbeat, steady and insistent.

Patrick smoothed a damp palm down the side of his costume, the unfamiliar richness of velvet and silk clinging like a second skin. The doublet was stiff across his shoulders, the boots heavy. Honestly, he felt less like a romantic lead and more like a very expensive, very anxious piece of upholstery. Yet, he felt buoyed by it, armored by centuries of theater tradition. His heart thudded in frantic sync with the orchestra's tuning notes bleeding faintly from the pit.

He found himself glancing sideways, searching. Dean stood just a few feet away, already dressed in his Romeo costume, velvet the color of dark sapphires cut to flatter his long frame. The jewel tones made his hair gleam, caught the edge of his jaw, and sharpened the hazel in his eyes until Patrick's stomach gave a dangerous lurch.

Patrick let out a short, unsteady laugh before whispering, "Jesus, how do you look even hotter than usual?"

Dean's mouth curved into a grin, small but sharp, his eyes flicking over Patrick with equal appraisal.

Patrick leaned in closer, voice a conspiratorial whisper: "If we weren't about to go onstage, I would do so many things to you right now."

Dean's laugh came low, steady, sliding straight through Patrick's skin. He caught Patrick's hand quickly, squeezed it once, and murmured back, "Then consider that your motivation. Survive tonight, and you can do whatever you like."

Patrick's face burned, but the heat in his chest steadied him more than any breathing exercise Diana had ever drilled into them. Nerves didn't vanish, but they shifted, becoming something sharper, something alive.

"You're nervous?" Dean asked softly, his thumb brushing the back of Patrick's knuckles. His voice was low, meant only for him.

"Terrified," Patrick admitted. His throat tightened as he tried to force humor into it. "Feels like I'm about to juggle flaming torches while tightrope walking over the Thames in Elizabethan boots. And these tights are surprisingly drafty."

Dean chuckled, and the sound grounded him instantly. "We'll jump together. You're brilliant. You're going to mesmerize them. Just remember, I'm right there with you. Always."

Patrick's chest clenched. He squeezed Dean's hand back, hard, eyes stinging with a sudden wave of gratitude. "Thank you."

The house lights dimmed another degree, the faint chatter of the audience cut to a hush. The sudden silence felt holy.

The overture began, haunting, a mournful violin entwined with low piano chords. The melody curled through the theater like smoke, delicate and aching, pulling everyone inward, preparing them for Verona's tragedy.

Patrick shut his eyes for one long, steadying breath. Then he opened them, lifted his chin, and stepped closer to the wings. Dean was beside him, close enough that their shoulders brushed.

The curtain rose.

The play leapt into motion: vibrant masks and flashing swords, laughter and feuds painted in bold colors. Patrick was carried into it, his body remembering every cue, every mark drilled in sweat and hours. But tonight was different. Every line he spoke rang truer, pulled from somewhere deeper. His Julius was no longer just a role; it was a vessel for all he had lived this summer, every fear and hope pressed into the poetry of Shakespeare's words.

When he and Dean first met eyes across the masked ball, the spark that leapt between them was not rehearsed. Patrick's breath caught behind the mask as if he were truly seeing him for the first time. Their hands found one another in the dance, movements once clumsy now fluid, a seamless ballet of recognition. It felt private even in front of hundreds of eyes.

By the time the balcony scene arrived, Patrick's nerves had transmuted into something electric. Perched above the stage in a wash of pale light, he spoke his lines with raw openness, the longing flowing out of him unchecked. Dean stood below, eyes never leaving his, voice low and fervent as he answered back. The world shrank until there was only this: two voices, two bodies, two hearts tumbling toward each other beneath the guise of Shakespeare.

And when the kiss came, it was no longer about rehearsals or stage directions. Patrick felt Dean's lips meet his, steady and sure, and for a moment he forgot the crowd entirely. The audience's collective gasp barely registered. It was a kiss for Julius and Romeo, but also, undeniably, for Patrick and Dean.

The kiss lingered even after they drew apart, both of

them dazed, the silence of the audience pressing heavy and awed. Then the play surged on, carrying them forward.

Each act blurred into the next, lines and cues unfurling like dominoes. Patrick spoke with a fluency he'd never quite reached in rehearsal, his voice carrying Julius's devotion and despair in equal measure. He felt his own heart crack open with every declaration, every plea. Dean answered with fire, his Romeo alive with reckless passion, a raw vulnerability beneath the swagger.

Their classmates fed off the energy too. Monty's Nurse drew belly laughs and sighs in the same breath; Jess's poise as Mercutio steadied the stage like a keel.

Even Bobby, the poor guy from group Lysander drafted in to play Paris after Jacob's unceremonious exit, managed to hold his own. Patrick patted him on the shoulder just before his entrance, whispering a fierce, "You got this," though Bobby looked like he was vibrating at a frequency that could shatter glass. Patrick briefly worried the poor guy might actually throw up on his boots, which would really ruin the tragic aesthetic. But Dean guided the fight with professional grace, making the duel look dangerous and sharp without ever actually putting the nervous replacement in harm's way. It gave the scene a frantic, desperate energy that actually worked.

Patrick barely registered the shifting lights, the costume changes, the sweat cooling and reappearing under layers of velvet. He was submerged, living inside Julius's tragic skin, every word he spoke braided with his own pulse. The edge between reality and performance disappeared.

The tragedy deepened. Shadows grew longer, voices harsher. Patrick felt himself unravel scene by scene, each step dragging Julius closer to the inevitable. His throat scraped raw from grief, his body ached from the intensity, but none of it mattered. The audience was with them; he could feel it in the silence, the collective breath, the tears being held back.

And then, the tomb.

The air turned glacial backstage as the scene shifted. Patrick lay among the cold stone props, pale makeup smudged by sweat, chest heaving as Julius delivered his last anguished words. Dean knelt beside him, trembling with a desperation so real Patrick felt his own heart split.

Dean's Romeo reached for the dagger, his hand shaking. The blade caught the light, cruel and silver. "Here's to my love," he said, voice breaking. He pressed the hilt to his chest, then lifted the cup to his lips. "O true apothecary," he whispered, his breath faltering as he drank. "Thy drugs are quick. Thus, with a kiss, I die."

He fell beside Patrick, the cup rolling from his hand, the silence of the theater shattering into a collective gasp.

Patrick's Julius stirred weakly, his eyes fluttering open to the sight of Romeo's still body. His trembling hand found the dagger beside them, the prop cold and slick with stage blood. He cradled Dean's face, his thumb brushing over the curve of his jaw as if trying to wake him.

"What's here?" Patrick breathed, voice low and shaking. "A dagger… O happy dagger." His grip tightened, his whole body trembling as the words left him. "This is thy sheath." He pressed the blade to his chest, eyes locked on Dean's. "There rust, and let me die."

He drove it home. His body arched once, then stilled, the light draining from his face as the stage lights dimmed to twilight.

The silence that followed was absolute. Not a cough, not a shuffle, only the faint echo of the violin from the pit, carrying the tragedy into stillness.

For a heartbeat, Patrick thought he might never rise again. The exhaustion, the emotional hollowing, felt too real. Then came the eruption, applause crashing like surf, a roar of voices breaking through the hush. The audience leapt to its feet, a wave of bodies and sound and stamping that rolled through the theater.

Patrick blinked into the light as the curtain fell and rose again for bows. Dean grabbed his hand, squeezing hard, their palms slick with sweat, their smiles wild with disbelief.

Patrick and Dean stepped forward together, side by side, bowing into the roar, the heat of it washing over them.

The applause still thundered in Patrick's bones long after they'd filed offstage. Backstage was chaos, costumes half-flung, actors sobbing into each other's arms, Garrett booming praise so loudly it rattled the scenery flats.

Patrick stood dazed, his chest still heaving, Dean's hand still clasped in his. Neither of them let go as the cast swirled around them.

"You were—" Dean started, then broke off, shaking his head like words weren't enough.

Patrick leaned close, whispering through the din. "So were you. God, Dean, I'm so proud of you. Not just for tonight but for everything. For being brave."

Dean's eyes softened, the noise fading for just a moment. He pressed his forehead to Patrick's. "You make it worth it."

Patrick hesitated, then squeezed Dean's hand tighter, his voice dropping to a fierce, tender whisper.

"Dean," he said. "I know you were scared. But you did it. And I bet your sister would be so proud of you right now."

Dean's breath hitched. For a second, the chaos of the room fell away. A sheen of tears rose in his eyes, bright and sudden, but he didn't look away. He just nodded, a small, trembling movement, and squeezed Patrick's hand tight.

"Thank you, Patrick," Dean said quietly.

Before Patrick could respond, Monty came crashing into them, arms wide, champagne already sloshing in his glass. "My tragic heroes!" he bellowed, nearly knocking them both over in a hug. "Romeo! Julius! You've killed me. I'll never recover. Put me in the ground with them, for I am undone!"

Jess dragged him back by his sleeve, rolling her eyes. "Ignore him. He's been swigging since the second bow. But honestly." She pulled Patrick into a fierce hug, then Dean. "You were breathtaking. That balcony scene? Half the front row was fanning themselves. And the kiss… Bloody hell. If I didn't know better, I'd say it wasn't acting."

Patrick flushed, laughing despite himself. Dean only smirked, tugging Patrick a little closer, his arm still looped casually around his waist.

Olivia appeared next, quieter than the rest, a glass of champagne in her hand. Her smile was soft but steady. "That was incredible," she said simply. Her gaze flicked between the two of them. She lifted her glass. "To Romeo and Julius."

"Thanks, Liv." Patrick clinked his cup gently against hers.

Before he could say more, Garrett swooped in, velvet scarf trailing like the wings of a dramatic bat, voice booming with delight. "Magnificent! Transcendent! You found the truth and bared it raw. You shook the rafters, my darlings. That kiss alone, electric. Unforgettable." His knowing glance lingered on Patrick and Dean, a sly twinkle in his eye, before he swept on to lavish praise on Monty, who promptly pretended to faint from flattery.

Diana wasn't far behind. She gathered Patrick and

Dean both into her arms, squeezing them fiercely. Her perfume clung to Patrick's collar as she whispered, "Magnificent, my loves. Absolutely magnificent. You made my heart sing." When she finally let go, her eyes shone with unshed tears.

The common room transformed into a carnival. Champagne corks popped, music blasted from someone's portable speaker, and actors danced in their costumes until the ruffs started to unravel. Monty led a rowdy chorus of "RADA! RADA!" while Jess insisted on harmonizing and Olivia tried to rein him in, laughing too much to succeed.

Patrick was spun in circles by classmates, kissed on the cheek by strangers, clapped on the back until he thought his ribs might crack. But through it all, Dean never strayed more than an arm's length away, his hand finding Patrick's again and again, anchoring him.

At last, when the chaos swelled too loud, Patrick tugged him gently toward the edge of the room. They ducked behind a towering palm in the corner, finding a sagging sofa half-hidden from view.

The noise softened to a muffled hum. Patrick sank down beside Dean, exhaustion crashing over him at last. Dean slung an arm around his shoulders, pulling him close, pressing a kiss to his temple.

Patrick let out a long, shaky breath. "We really did it."

"We did," Dean said. He pulled back just enough to look Patrick in the eye, his thumb tracing the line of his jaw. "But the best part?"

"What?"

"We get to wake up tomorrow," Dean whispered. "We don't have to die in the tomb. We get to keep going."

Patrick smiled, a true, bone-deep smile that felt brighter than any spotlight.

"Patrick whispered. "Yes, we do."

Patrick leaned back, letting the celebration blur into color and sound. He thought about the plane ticket he'd bought months ago, the terrified dancer who had boarded a flight with nothing but a suitcase and a desperate need to prove himself. He had come here to find his footing as an actor, to prove he could be more than just a dancer in the background. He had done that. He had taken the lead.

But he'd found something else, too. He glanced at Dean, who was watching him with that same steady, quiet adoration.

Patrick closed his eyes, feeling full of love, of exhaustion, and of something that would last long after the lights went out.

CHAPTER 18

The final days of the RADA summer program unfolded like the last bars of a symphony: bittersweet, triumphant, and touched with melancholy. The high of their opening-night success lingered in every corridor and common room, woven into the very air of Gower Street, but with it came the quiet ache of imminent goodbyes.

There were farewell pints in crowded pubs, hugs traded in dim hallways, and the kind of promises about staying in touch that everyone meant in the moment but not all would keep.

Patrick felt it most in the little moments: Monty retelling a botched quick-change with such dramatic flourish the whole table collapsed in laughter, Jess bursting into spontaneous Shakespeare at the bar, Olivia slipping him a wry smile over her glass like she was watching the whole thing with quiet fondness. The air smelled of stale beer and ambition, a strangely fitting perfume for their makeshift troupe.

But for Patrick, the ache was dulled by a steady undercurrent of certainty. He was not saying goodbye to Dean. Not this time. Every glance, every lingering brush of hands, every late-night whisper about what came next carried the same promise. This was not an ending. It was the beginning of something bigger, something real.

The official end of the program came with a ceremony. RADA's historic main hall, usually echoing with rehearsals and laughter, had been transformed into something hushed and reverent. Sunlight streamed through tall, arched windows and scattered gold across the polished floor. Folding chairs creaked under the weight of nerves. Dust motes drifted lazily in the shafts of light like tiny spirits marking the moment.

Patrick sat beside Dean, their hands linked beneath the seats, a secret thread of connection in the hush.

Garrett and Diana stood at the front. Between them sat a simple podium dressed with a modest spray of flowers, but even that looked ceremonial under the soaring windows. Garrett cleared his throat, and the low hum of whispers cut off instantly. He never needed to raise his voice. His presence alone was enough to command stillness.

"This summer has been," Garrett began, drawing the words out like he was already holding them on stage, "a crucible. You have all bled and burned for your craft," he said gravely, then allowed a wry smile. "And occasionally bled for your sword choreography, but that's another matter." His mouth twitched into the faintest of smiles. "And for that, I am proud."

Diana leaned in then, her tone gentler, her words wrapping the room in warmth. "You've grown—each of you. We've watched you risk, fail, rise, and risk again. That is theater. That is life."

Patrick's chest swelled at her words, his throat tight. He squeezed Dean's hand, felt the squeeze back, and drew in a breath that tasted of dust, sunlight, and hope. Because beyond all the speeches, beyond the polite applause, was what everyone in the room was waiting for. The results.

When Garrett shuffled the stack of papers on the podium, the tension rose like a tide and filled the space until Patrick swore he could hear it ringing in his ears.

Garrett adjusted his glasses with deliberate slowness, savoring the moment the way only a lifelong man of theater could. The shuffle of papers was louder than thunder in the still hall. Twenty-five students sat rigid, hearts thundering, the future balanced on a knife's edge.

"And now," Garrett said at last, his smile widening, "to those of you who will be invited to continue your training with us for the MA Theatre Lab program…"

The silence sharpened to a blade. Patrick's stomach flipped so violently he thought he might be sick. His fingers clenched tighter around Dean's under the chair until their knuckles pressed white.

Garrett began to read names. Each one was met with a ripple of applause, cheers from friends, muffled sighs of relief. Patrick tried to keep his breathing steady and tried not to count how many spots had already been announced.

"Dean Clarke."

The name dropped like a stone into still water. Patrick's whole body lit up. He turned instantly and saw the way Dean's jaw unclenched, how his shoulders sagged with released tension, and felt a rush of fierce pride. He squeezed Dean's hand so hard it almost hurt, a grin breaking across his face before he could stop it. Dean met his gaze, eyes gleaming, and let out a soft, incredulous laugh.

"Jessica Montez."

Jess let out a shriek so loud it made half the hall jump, then slapped both hands over her mouth before dissolving into giggles. Patrick twisted in his chair to see her beaming through tears.

"Montgomery Price."

Monty leapt to his feet with a theatrical gasp, hands clasped to his chest like he had just been knighted. The applause turned into laughter as he executed a full bow toward Garrett, then spun to blow kisses at the rest of the students.

Garrett continued, his voice crisp:

"And Patrick O'Connell."

The words hit like fireworks, like a wave crashing over him. Patrick gasped, his grin splitting wider, tears stinging at the back of his eyes.

He had done it. He had done it. He wasn't just a chorus boy from New York anymore, hoping to be seen. He was in. He was staying. He and Dean were staying together.

Dean pulled him into a quick, hard hug, the kind you were not supposed to share in such a formal setting, but neither of them cared. Patrick felt laughter bubble up out of him, unstoppable.

The final names were read, applause rippling in waves until Garrett folded the list away with a decisive snap. The tension broke into chatter, laughter, and scattered tears. Patrick sat still for a moment, just breathing, Dean's hand still twined in his.

It was Olivia who reached them first, slipping past rows of chairs to pull Patrick into a hug. "Congratulations," she said softly, though her smile wobbled. "You both were incredible. Truly. You deserve this."

"Thanks, Liv," Patrick whispered, squeezing her tightly.

Then Jacob approached. For once there was no swagger in his step, no smirk plastered on his face. His hands were jammed into his pockets, and he looked uncomfortable. Vulnerable.

He stopped in front of them, shifting his weight.

"Listen," he began, eyes darting between them. "I've been…an ass. Toward you, Clarke. And toward you, O'Connell." His voice cracked slightly, but he pushed on. "I shouldn't have thrown that punch. It was cheap. And O'Connell... You stepped up. You earned the role. I respect that."

Patrick blinked, startled by the honesty. Dean straightened slowly, watching Jacob like he was not sure if this was some elaborate bit.

Jacob rubbed the back of his neck, grimacing. "I'm…sorry. Truly. You were both brilliant in the play. And you earned this. Both of you."

He hesitated, glancing toward where Garrett was chatting with Diana. "I actually had a chat with Garrett this morning," Jacob admitted, his voice quieter. "He ripped me a new one—rightfully so. But...he said I could come back next summer. Try the program again. If I can prove I've actually grown up a bit."

Patrick raised his eyebrows, surprised but pleased. "That's great, Jacob. Everyone deserves a second chance."

For a beat, silence stretched. Then Dean extended his hand, quiet but firm. "Thank you," he said.

Jacob hesitated only a second before clasping it. When he turned to Patrick, Patrick gave him a small, genuine smile and nodded. "Apology accepted."

Relief flickered across Jacob's face, and then he melted back into the throng.

Patrick turned to Dean, whose lips curved in something halfway between disbelief and amusement. "Well," Dean murmured, "miracles do happen."

Patrick laughed, the sound shaky with relief. He leaned into Dean, the compass at Dean's neck glinting in the sunlight. For the first time all summer, the path ahead felt wide open.

The pub was bedlam in the best possible way. Pints foamed over onto the sticky tables. Voices rose in raucous toasts. Jess was on the third retelling of her near-death experience during the duel scene, waving a pool cue like it was Excalibur.

Monty howled with laughter, clutching his side. "You tripped over your own cloak, Jess."

"It was theater," Jess corrected, swaying dramatically and nearly upending someone's drink. "High art. My tumble will be remembered for generations."

Olivia groaned, but her smile betrayed her. She leaned against the bar, sipping prosecco while pretending not to be entertained.

Jacob caught Patrick's eye across the table and lifted his glass in mock salute. Patrick rolled his eyes but clinked back anyway, the gesture easier than he had expected.

Jess came careening over, curls bouncing as she threw her arms around Patrick's neck. "You were brilliant tonight." She kissed his cheek noisily before swinging around to grab Dean in the same crushing embrace. "And you. Don't think you're escaping me now. You're family, both of you. Sorry, no refunds."

Dean flushed but smiled, sliding his arm around Patrick's waist once she released him. Monty swooped in next, sloshing beer dangerously as he attempted to drape himself across all three of them.

"My beloved companions," Monty declared, voice booming like a proclamation. "Let us swear eternal brotherhood. Annual reunions. Cheap drinks. Bad karaoke."

"Sit down before you fall into the dartboard again," Olivia scolded, but she was laughing too.

At some point Monty collapsed into a chair and dragged Jess down with him. Instead of pushing him off, she stayed tucked against his side, both of them flushed from laughter and drink. Monty whispered something in her ear that made her snort so hard she nearly spilled her pint.

Patrick, watching from across the table, arched a brow and caught Jess's eye. He mouthed a silent, exaggerated Really?

Jess smirked and gave the tiniest shrug, as if to say, "What can you do?" Then she leaned more comfortably against Monty's shoulder, her fingers idly tracing the rim of her glass.

Patrick shook his head, biting back a grin. Dean, noticing, leaned down and murmured, "Looks like someone else had a summer subplot."

"Apparently," Patrick whispered back, before raising his pint in a mock toast toward Jess. She rolled her eyes but clinked her glass against Monty's with a little flourish, playing up the moment just to make Patrick laugh harder.

The whole table erupted again when Monty tried to kiss the back of Jess's hand with regal gallantry, missed, and ended up nearly knocking her beer into Jacob's lap.

Patrick laughed until his sides hurt, warmth buzzing through him, not just from the drinks but from the sheer, improbable joy of it all.

Dean's hand brushed his under the table, fingers linking easily. In the midst of all the chaos, the clatter of glasses, Monty's booming voice, Jess's wicked cackles, Patrick felt an anchor, steady and warm.

He reached into his pocket, his thumb hovering over the screen. He couldn't keep this to just this room. He opened the group chat with his mom and aunts—*The Golden Girls.*

He typed quickly: *I got in! Accepted to the MA Program. London is home for a while longer.*

The response was immediate.

Mom: *MY BABY!!! I KNEW IT! I'm crying! Tell the King I said hello!*

Aunt Therese: *Oh my god! Congrats! Do we need to curtsy when you visit??*

Aunt Ann: *Yay! We are so proud. Bring home a prince!*

Patrick snorted, shaking his head. He switched to his chat with LaShelle and Eli.

Made the cut. Staying in London. Send shipping crates.

Three seconds later, LaShelle responded.

LaShelle: *SCREAMING!! I am already looking at flights. I expect a full royal tour.*

Eli: *Never had a doubt, Patty boy!! Proud of you! Now go celebrate with Loverboy ;-)*

Patrick smiled down at the screen, his heart full. He tilted the phone so Dean could see.

"They seem calm," Dean noted dryly, eyeing the wall of texts.

"Oh, this is restrained," Patrick laughed, slipping the phone back into his pocket. "Wait until they actually meet you."

Eventually, chairs scraped back, and coats were thrown on, the crowd beginning to thin. Olivia hugged them both tight and pressed a kiss to Patrick's cheek. "Proud of you two," she said warmly before slipping off into the night.

That left Monty and Jess, still tucked against each other, flushed with drink and laughter. Patrick bent down, pulling Jess into a quick hug, then Monty. "We'll see you two soon," he teased, raising a brow at the way they were leaning together.

Jess only smirked, shrugging as if to say caught red-handed, while Monty lifted his pint in solemn agreement. "Reunion at Gig's. Mark it down."

Patrick laughed, then felt Dean's hand squeeze his. He turned and found hazel eyes warm and steady.

"Ready to go?" Dean murmured.

Patrick nodded. They waved one last time to their friends and stepped out into the cool London night, leaving behind the raucous warmth of the pub for something quieter, something that belonged just to them.

The next day Patrick had a surprise in store for Dean. He wanted to give him a gift that was not just a thing but an experience, something that spoke to their shared love of art, and to the quiet, profound beauty that resided within Dean's soul.

He had managed to procure two tickets to a sold-out Royal Ballet production of *Romeo and Juliet* at the iconic Royal Opera House. It took an unholy amount of internet stalking, a slightly embarrassing phone call in his best *I'm-a-very-serious-theater-professional* voice, and a desperate plea to a surprisingly helpful ticket agent who seemed to appreciate his dramatic flair.

Patrick kept his plan a secret, hinting only at a special night out.

He dressed carefully, choosing a dark, well-tailored suit that felt both sophisticated and subtly celebratory, a stark contrast to the casual rehearsal clothes he had lived in for weeks. He spent an extra few minutes on his hair, trying to achieve that effortlessly disheveled look that Dean seemed to master so naturally, a small, self-conscious effort to match Dean's inherent elegance.

Dean, ever easygoing, simply smiled and followed Patrick's lead, his hand casually linked in Patrick's as they navigated the bustling, vibrant streets of Covent Garden. The air was alive with the chatter of theater-goers, the distant strains of street performers, and the intoxicating aroma of fresh flowers from the market mingling with the faint, sweet scent of roasting nuts.

As they walked, Dean bumped his shoulder gently against Patrick's. "You know what this means, right? The MA program?"

Patrick glanced at him. "That we have to buy more overpriced textbooks?"

Dean laughed. "It means you're stuck in London. With me. For at least another year."

Patrick's smile turned soft, undeniable. "I think I can handle that."

Patrick felt a giddy anticipation bubbling in his chest, a mixture of nerves and pure joy. Dean looked impossibly handsome in his own dark suit, the crisp white shirt a striking contrast to his dark hair, which as always, had that one perfect piece falling charmingly over his eye.

When they finally stood before the majestic façade of the Royal Opera House, its grand columns and imposing architecture illuminated against the twilight sky and casting long, dramatic shadows, Dean's eyes widened in genuine awe.

"Patrick," Dean breathed, a soft, astonished whisper, his gaze sweeping over the building. "What are we doing here? Are we just admiring the architecture? Because it is truly magnificent, but I feel wildly underdressed for mere admiration."

He turned to Patrick, a question in his eyes, a hint of playful confusion but beneath it, a deep and genuine curiosity.

Patrick grinned and pulled the embossed envelope from his jacket pocket with a flourish, a theatrical gesture he knew Dean would appreciate.

"Hardly, my dear. Tonight we immerse ourselves in culture. Specifically, in a certain tragedy of star-crossed lovers, but this time with significantly less dialogue and far more elegant leaps, pirouettes, and dramatic falls."

He handed Dean the tickets, savoring the slow dawning of understanding in his face.

Dean's eyes widened even further, then crinkled at the corners as a slow, incredulous smile spread across his lips. It reached his eyes and made them sparkle with pure, unadulterated joy.

"*Romeo and Juliet?* The Royal Ballet? Patrick, this is absolutely incredible. You didn't have to do this. How did you even manage this?"

His delight warmed Patrick's heart more than any summer sun, a profound appreciation that made all the effort worthwhile. Dean squeezed his hand, a silent thank you that spoke volumes.

"Let's just say it involved a certain American charm and a very shameless phone call to the box office," Patrick teased, gently squeezing Dean's hand back, his smile widening. "Either way, our red velvet seats await. And I hear the pre-show champagne is divine, a perfect prelude to an evening of tragic beauty."

He led Dean towards the grand entrance, feeling a lightness in his step, a profound happiness that settled deep in his soul.

Stepping inside the Royal Opera House felt like entering another world entirely, a gilded, hushed realm of opulence and anticipation.

The grand foyer, with its towering ceilings, intricate gold leaf, and sweeping staircases, hummed with the murmur of elegantly dressed patrons. The air was thick with the scent of old theater: polished wood, fresh flowers, expensive cologne. Heady and intoxicating.

They found their seats, nestled comfortably in the plush red velvet, offering a perfect view of the stage. The ornate proscenium arch, adorned with cherubs and gilded garlands, framed the vast space like a living painting waiting to begin.

Patrick leaned back, a contented sigh escaping him, feeling Dean's warmth beside him. He glanced sideways. Dean's gaze was fixed on the stage, eyes wide with childlike wonder, his whole body alight with quiet anticipation.

The house lights dimmed. A collective hush fell.

The orchestra swelled, Prokofiev's score filling the hall with its sweeping, devastating melodies. The violins rose in mournful beauty, brass cut sharp and commanding, woodwinds breathed fragile longing. Each note wrapped around them like smoke and pulled them under.

From the first haunting bars, Patrick and Dean were lost. The dancers moved with breathtaking grace, their bodies telling a story of passion, conflict, and heartbreak with every fluid gesture, every leap, every turn.

Patrick's gaze drifted not to the stage but to Dean. The furrow of his brow during a complicated sequence. The soft gasp that escaped him during a pas de deux. The way a single tear slid silently down his cheek. Dean wore his heart openly here, vulnerable in the dark, and Patrick felt undone by the beauty of it.

He reached out, their hands finding each other in the dimness, fingers intertwining as if they had always belonged that way. Dean's thumb brushed gently over Patrick's knuckles, a simple rhythm of reassurance.

Patrick looked at Dean, who offered a tear-filled, understanding smile, both of them still caught in the ballet's spell. As the curtain fell and applause rose around them, their own story was only just beginning.

Outside, the city shimmered under the hush of late summer, the streets humming with life and possibility. The glow from the theater spilled across the pavement, painting their shadows gold. Dean reached for his hand, their fingers sliding together in a slow, deliberate intertwine—more promise than touch, more vow than gesture. The world seemed to still around it.

Patrick looked at him, the man who had changed everything. He had found his counterpart. He had rewritten the ending.

Standing in the golden glow of the theater, Patrick thought of the line they'd once spoken beneath the heat of stage lights, never knowing how true it would become:

"This bud of love, by summer's ripening breath, may prove a beauteous flower when next we meet."

ACKNOWLEDGMENTS

Several years ago, I thought I might write a book, something funny and chaotic about love and misadventure in New York. I shelved it for later, as we often do with the things that scare us most.

In 2019, that "later" finally arrived. I had the incredible opportunity to attend a summer program at RADA in London, a life-changing experience. It was there that I met Jordy, one of my now best friends. I also met an extraordinary group of actors and teachers who left a lasting impact on me.

So first, to Jordy, thank you for being you and for being such an important part of my life. To my fellow Fortune group members, our instructor, Gary, and the rest of the wonderful people I met that summer: you were all part of the inspiration for this book.

Much of what you've read is drawn from my life. While Patrick is fictional, this story is a love letter to the moments that have shaped me: the loves and losses, the career highs and heartbreaks, and the cities that have influenced me: New York, Scranton, and London. It is also a tribute to my family, my friends, and all the nerdy passions I hold dear.

To Katie, Gia, Ebony, Samantha, Elizabeth, Jestina, Jeanne, Margaret, Bridget, Amy, Amanda, Jennifer, Kim, Rachel, Charlotte, and so many other incredible women who have let me be my full, ridiculous self without judgment and have supported me every step of the way, I can't thank you enough.

To my dear friend and fellow author Colleen, thank you for your guidance, patience, and encouragement throughout this entire process. I will never forget it.

To my editor, Cameron, for making this book even more special. I am so grateful for your brilliant insight and for believing in this book.

To my cover designer, Gowtham, for the beautiful art that brought my characters to life.

To every professor, performing arts teacher, and mentor who helped me find my voice and believe in it, thank you.

To the men who were chapters in my life, thank you for the memories, the lessons, and yes, even the heartbreaks. You were all part of writing this story, whether you meant to be or not.

To my close friends of many years, anyone who has ever supported me, or who has just been there in some way, thank you.

And to anyone who has ever caused me pain or rooted for me to fail, believe it or not, you have kept me going. You gave me something to push against, and that is its own kind of gift.

To my Aunt Mair, thank you for your constant support and love. You have taught me to lead with kindness, and I am endlessly grateful.

To my Aunt Tish, thank you for being my inspiration, my travel buddy, and for introducing me to the arts. So much of what I do is possible because of you.

To my mother, my biggest supporter, my anchor, and my heart, thank you for standing beside me every step of the way. You are my rock, and I hope I have made you proud. I love you.

And finally, to my sweet dog Alfie, you sat beside me through every word of this book. You can't read this, but I'll read it to you later and give you all the kisses.

ABOUT THE AUTHOR

Michael McILwee is a performer and author who has appeared in productions such as *Phantom*, *A Chorus Line*, and *The Music Man*. He holds a BFA from The New School and an MA from NYU. A lifelong *Star Wars* fan and proud nerd, Michael was born and raised in Scranton, Pennsylvania, and now divides his time between New York and Los Angeles with his dog Alfie. *A Summer with Dean* is his first novel. Website: www.michaelmcilwee.com